NIGHTTRAP

Praise for the DARKSIDE series:

"Enough hellish mystery to have you drooling
for the next in the series".
Observer

"An exciting romp"
Daily Telegraph

"Wild and gripping ... brilliant"
Sunday Express

"Atmospheric"
Independent

"Brilliant"
Times Educational Supplement

"This is a real cracker! The thrills and
chills come thick and fast"
Gateway Monthly

"Full of spine-chilling characters
and stomach-turning action"
Herald Express

"It's got more terror and thrills than
you could get your fangs into"
Liverpool Echo

Also by Tom Becker

Darkside
Lifeblood

DARKSIDE

Tom Becker

NIGHTTRAP

SCHOLASTIC

First published in 2008 by Scholastic Children's Books
An imprint of Scholastic Ltd
Euston House, 24 Eversholt Street
London, NW1 1DB, UK
Registered office: Westfield Road, Southam, Warwickshire, CV47 0RA
SCHOLASTIC and associated logos are trademarks and or registered trademarks of
Scholastic Inc.

Text copyright © CPI Publishing Solutions, 2008
The right of Tom Becker to be identified as the
author of this work has been asserted by him.
Cover illustration © Studio Spooky, 2008

ISBN 978 1407 10287 0

A CIP catalogue record for this book is
available from the British Library

Printed in the UK by CPI Bookmarque, Croydon, CR0 4TD
Papers used by Scholastic Children's Books are made
from wood grown in sustainable forests.

1 3 5 7 9 10 8 6 4 2

www.scholastic.co.uk/zone

Prologue

August, in a city gasping for breath. The heat had wrapped thick, sweaty fingers around London, and was squeezing mercilessly. Choked streets pleaded in vain for a breeze. Trapped inside stuffy offices and airless tube trains, Londoners sweltered and roasted. Those unable to escape the city made for parks and gardens, and the shade beneath tree branches and sun umbrellas, but the heat sapped life from everything. Down by the riverfront, the Thames slumped lifelessly against the Embankment.

Deep in the bowels of a West London police station, Police Sergeant Charlie Wilson tugged at his collar and stared at the suspect in front of him with mounting disbelief. For a criminal mastermind, this was a singularly unusual figure. He had been in some sort of fight, and there was an ugly swelling on the back of his head. His eyes were wild and he fidgeted impatiently, as though he was late for an important appointment. Since waking up handcuffed to a hospital bed, the only thing he had said was his name. None of which would have been that strange, but for the fact that the suspect could not have been more than fifteen or sixteen years old.

Wilson didn't know what to make of it. At twenty-four, he wasn't that much older than the lad himself. He had only been in the force for a year, and nothing in training had prepared him for this. He scratched at a damp armpit and tried again.

"Look, Kevin, we can sit here all day if you want. Tomorrow too. It's not like you're going anywhere."

He paused, hoping for a reply. The tape recorder hummed in the silence.

"This isn't shoplifting, son. This is *serious*."

Kevin shrugged, and looked down at the floor. Wilson had dealt before with young lads who acted tough, but there was something different about this one. He was so distant, so disengaged, it was as if they were barely in the same room.

It was clearly going to be a long day. Wilson's mouth was parched and he had already finished off his jug of water. The boy hadn't asked for any, and Wilson was worried that if he went out for a refill he would look weak. If only it wasn't so damn hot!

He was just about to try a sterner approach when the door to Interview Room B creaked open, and in slipped the crumpled figure of Detective Carmichael. Wilson's eyes widened with surprise. A small, hunchbacked man squeezed into a cheap suit, the detective was an unlikely legend on the force. He shuffled round the police station like a tramp, rarely speaking to any of his colleagues. Yet, time and time again, this unassuming figure had cracked high-profile cases that had stumped other coppers. By rights, he should have made Super by now, but there was something about Carmichael that unsettled his colleagues. To everyone's relief, he seemed happy to remain a detective, albeit one who could pick and choose his cases. And today he had chosen Wilson's.

Detective Carmichael sized up the room with one swift glance and collapsed into a chair. Rubbing an eye wearily, he nodded at Wilson.

"Morning, Sergeant," he said softly. "Thought you might appreciate a helping hand on this case. Why don't you tell me what's going on?"

Wilson shuffled his notes, and replied with a dry mouth:

"Right . . . yes, sir. Well, in the early hours of this morning, an armed police unit responded to reports of gunfire and a burning vehicle outside an address in Kensington. Having gained access to the building, they found evidence of a break-in, and bloodstains indicating a violent struggle. The owner of the residence was nowhere to be seen. In fact, the only person left on the premises was the suspect here, who was lying unconscious on the floor of a high-security vault in the basement. He was clutching this, sir." He showed his superior a photograph of a glittering stone, an ice-blue sapphire. "Experts reckon it's worth a couple of million."

Detective Carmichael raised an eyebrow and turned to

the young boy. "Not bad for a lad your age. Trying to impress a girlfriend, were we?"

Kevin snorted humourlessly. Secretly, Wilson was relieved that the vaunted Carmichael's entrance hadn't improved the lad's attitude.

"The suspect is refusing to cooperate, sir," he cut in helpfully. "All we've been able to get out of him is his name."

The detective gave the boy a long, thoughtful stare. Then he leant forward and said, almost in a whisper, "I bet you didn't give your real name, though, did you, Jonathan?"

The boy looked up sharply, a shocked expression on his face. Carmichael chuckled, shaking his head.

"For a clever lad, you must think we're awfully stupid. Did you think we'd just take your word for it? Did you not think we might run your photo through a database? What do you think this is, son – the nineteenth century?"

The detective's mouth may have still been creased in a smile, but his eyes were deadly serious now. He stared at the boy, challenging him. Jonathan held his gaze, but didn't say anything.

Wilson was lost.

"Sir?" he ventured.

The sound of his voice broke the spell in the room. Carmichael turned back to him, his mouth twitching with amusement.

"This is a very special day, Sergeant. We're interviewing a ghost."

"I . . . I don't understand, sir."

Carmichael settled back in his chair. "Young Jonathan Starling here was kidnapped in central London a year ago. Despite a huge manhunt, he was never found. Suddenly the investigation was closed down and no one – not one family member, not one friend, Wilson – argued or asked any questions. It was as if everyone just . . . forgot about him. And now, out of the blue, here he is again! The only suspect in an attempted multi-million-pound robbery." He smiled again at Jonathan. "Whatever your story is, son, I can't wait to hear it."

The boy sat back and folded his arms obstinately.

"Listen to me, Jonathan," Wilson said, struggling to keep up. "You can't have got into that vault on your own. That place was built like a fortress. Someone was with you – an adult, criminals. Whoever you're trying to protect, you need to think about whether it's worth keeping silent. They've done a runner and left you to face the music. Where are they now?"

"I don't know." Jonathan spoke up for the first time, a note of determination in his voice. "But I'll find out."

Wilson made an exasperated noise. The boy seemed determined to be unhelpful.

"Keep this up, and the only place you'll be going is juvenile prison. Why don't you just tell us what's been going on?"

"What's the point?" Jonathan shot back. "You won't believe a word I say anyway."

"You'd be surprised by some of the things we've heard in this room. As long as it's the truth, son, then that's all right."

"Where've you been, Jonathan?" asked Detective Carmichael.

"Away," he replied defiantly.

"Have you been OK?"

"I've been fine. It was when I came back *here* that all the trouble started."

Jonathan paused, seemingly unsure of what to say next. Wilson gave him a look of encouragement.

"Go on."

Jonathan sighed, and began to talk.

1

Jonathan Starling was looking for trouble.

At first glance, most people wouldn't have realized this. Trudging round a North London shopping centre, his shoelaces trailing after him across the tiled floor, Jonathan cut an awkward figure. His body was crammed into a school uniform that was at least one size too small for his gangly frame. His hair was a tangled battleground of warring strands. A battered school bag hung limply from one shoulder. A keen observer might have wondered why the schoolboy wasn't in lessons at this time of the afternoon, but no one was watching him that closely. In fact, no one was watching him at all.

It was all very frustrating. Jonathan had spent over an hour in the shopping centre trying to get noticed. In the huge sports shop, he had dribbled a football around the aisles, playing one-twos off the wall, but no one had come over to stop him. He had loitered in the music store, trailing a hand over the racks of CDs and DVDs, without receiving a single suspicious glance. He had glared at every security guard he had seen, but they studiously ignored him. He was invisible again.

It had been a month since Jonathan had left the cobbled streets of Darkside and returned to everyday London. Moving back hadn't been easy. The problem was, Jonathan had changed. There had been times in Darkside when he would have given anything to feel safe and bored. But now, confronted with the routine of his old life, he was desperate for a buzz, that wave of adrenalin that had carried him from one scrape to another. It was as if somehow he *needed* fear now.

Even with the air conditioning on, the shopping centre was simmering with the heat of early summer. Gentle acoustic music drifted down from hidden speakers. Jonathan looked around at the milling shoppers with disdain. How could they not know? How could they be so blind? If he stood very still and closed his eyes, Jonathan could feel Darkside's presence – a giant, malevolent octopus hidden away in the depths of London, its alleyway tentacles stretching out into the city. Somewhere close by, he knew there would be a secret trapdoor or a dank sewer that could take him back there. Jonathan wondered whether his senses could guide him back. After all, he was half-Darksider: the borough was in his blood.

But he couldn't go back, not yet. He had promised.

In some ways, it was incredible that danger had become such a distant memory. Having crossed two of the most powerful men on Darkside – the vampiric banker Vendetta, and the heir to the Darkside throne Lucien Ripper – Jonathan and his ally Carnegie had prepared themselves for a tidal wave of vengeful violence. For weeks the wereman spent the nights in his lodgings sat in a chair, his eyes fixed on the door, his hand on a weapon. In the next room, Jonathan woke every time a windowpane rattled or a floorboard creaked.

As time went on, however, they slowly realized that no one was coming for them. The *Darkside Informer* had seen to that. In a series of explosive articles, it not only revealed Lucien and Marianne's true identity as the children of Thomas Ripper, but also the fact that Lucien had murdered his brother James twelve years beforehand. Even by Darkside's high standards, this was considered a foul deed. With his cover blown, and day after day of lurid headlines screaming for his blood, Lucien had been forced to disappear from the face of the rotten borough. Although Carnegie had made enquiries in his usual robust style, no one seemed to know where the Ripper had gone to lick his wounds. And, although one night Jonathan had seen Vendetta's car roaring down the Grand, scattering horses and passers-by like ninepins, the vampire had also withdrawn from the public eye. The streets of Darkside still provided a riotous stage for its cast of treacherous and murderous characters, and danger lurked round every corner, but that was normal for the borough. Eventually Carnegie ended his night-time vigils, and Jonathan's sleep became unbroken.

If anything, the wereman seemed more unnerved by the quiet than by the prospect of violence. He stalked down the Grand, his eyes furtively wary, glowering at anyone foolish enough to meet his gaze.

"It's not right, boy," he muttered through clenched teeth. "This is Darkside. You don't cross people and get away with it. People here don't forgive and forget."

Jonathan didn't know what to make of it. Though he was relieved that their lives didn't appear to be in any immediate danger, the search for his mother had reached another dead end. His encounter with Lucien had only reinforced his belief that Theresa Starling was still alive somewhere in Darkside, but the Ripper seemed the only person who might know where. With his disappearance, the trail to Theresa went stone cold.

In the end, it was Carnegie who forced him to face facts. The wereman had dragged Jonathan to the meat locker of Col's butcher's shop, where he ravaged a joint of beef while the boy stamped his feet in a futile attempt to keep warm. When the beast within him was sated, Carnegie wiped away a fleck of gristle from his cheek with his shirtsleeve and shot Jonathan a sideways glance.

"Look, boy," he said eventually, "I've been thinking things over, and I've decided it's time you went back to Lightside."

"What? Why?"

"There's nothing here for you. The only lead to Theresa has dried up. Until we find Lucien, we can't do anything."

"Something will turn up!" Jonathan protested. "It has to! And until then, I can help you with your cases. I've done all right so far, haven't I?"

"You've been fine. But I don't need a partner. I only agreed to look after you while Alain was ill, and he's better now." Carnegie's eyes narrowed. "You're not on holiday, and I'm not your uncle, boy."

"This isn't a holiday for me! I'm part-Darksider, remember?"

"You're part-Lightsider too, and right now, that's where you belong. It's been too long since you saw your dad. You need to go and spend some time with him. I'll keep digging over here. If I find out anything about Lucien or your mum, I'll come and get you. We'll start again then. But wait until I come for you. Deal?"

Jonathan spent the rest of the day alternately cajoling and arguing with the wereman, but only succeeded in turning his mood increasingly sour. Eventually Carnegie lost patience and snarled at Jonathan to be silent. That evening, the two friends parted company at a crossing point back to London without exchanging another word.

So now he was back on Lightside, trying to get used to televisions and computers and mobile phones and all the other technological gizmos that had seemed important a long time ago. His favourite songs sounded strange, and films bored him. No special effects could match what he had seen.

This wasn't to say that life was all bad. It was great being back with his dad again. Alain Starling was nearly fully recovered from his latest darkening – an illness caused by the time he had spent in Darkside many years ago. He was a different man from the distant figure who had brought Jonathan up. There were still times he would lapse into silence and stare off into the middle distance, but now a question or a stupid joke could snap him out of his reverie. Jonathan knew that the fact that Theresa remained missing caused Alain great pain, but he was more positive than before. On long, rambling walks on Hampstead Heath and through Regent's Park, the two Starlings concocted various wild schemes to pick up the trail and somehow bring her home.

Occasionally Alain would adopt a serious expression and threaten to enrol Jonathan in a new school in the autumn – "Darkside's all very well, but you've got to finish your education" – but both of them knew that his heart wasn't really in it. Alain understood better than anyone what it felt like to dream of returning to the rotten borough. They spent evenings together leafing through the Lightside books he had collected that contained secret, cryptic references to Darkside. At those moments, Jonathan knew deep down that Carnegie had been right to send him back, but it didn't stop him hoping that the wereman would soon shamble into view and take him back to Darkside.

"Excuse me, son?"

12

A tall policeman stepped out into Jonathan's path, interrupting his train of thought. He frowned at him in a manner that Jonathan recognized all too well.

"Is there a reason why you're not in school?"

Jonathan beamed at the man.

"Absolutely none. What are you going to do about it?"

This is more like it! Jonathan thought to himself as he hared across the concourse and scrambled up the escalators, two steps at a time. In the past, he would have avoided a chase in such a public place, but this was different. This was fun. His body had smoothly shifted into gear, grateful for the rush of adrenalin. Looking back over his shoulder, Jonathan saw that the policeman was already blowing hard and his cheeks were red. He wasn't in good enough shape for this chase.

Swerving through the crowds on autopilot, Jonathan raced along the upper level of the shopping centre, past a fast-food restaurant. He had almost reached the automatic doors at the end of the wide walkway, and freedom, when he saw a pair of security guards moving out from the doorway of a clothing shop. One of them looked straight at Jonathan, speaking urgently into a walkie-talkie. Great. *Now* they noticed him.

The situation was getting serious. There was a real danger he was going to get trapped. Jonathan took a sharp left and hurtled into a department store, knifing past shelves of ready meals and racks of women's clothes. He was moving so quickly and so quietly that most of the shoppers didn't seem to notice him. Behind him, he could hear the commotion of pursuit, the angry rattling of hangers as larger, heavier men crashed into them. Jonathan veered away from the cash desks and was urgently looking for a staircase or a doorway when his heart leapt. There was a fire exit in the wall right in front of him!

Jonathan crashed through the door and came out blinking into the bright sunshine of the car park. Without a pause he went ducking and weaving in between the gleaming machines, marking out a labyrinthine trail. He heard the sound of footfalls pounding out on to the tarmac, but Jonathan knew he was safe now. They'd never be able to find him amongst all these cars.

When he reached the far corner of the car park, Jonathan crouched down behind a blue convertible to catch his breath. Peering round the front of the bonnet, he caught sight of his three pursuers holding an irate conference several rows away from him. The policeman jabbed a finger at one of the security guards before stalking back inside the shopping centre.

Jonathan sat down and leant against the car, taking long, deep breaths. All too quickly, the adrenalin drained out of his system, and the familiar feeling of emptiness returned. He was just about to slip away and make for home when a hand reached out from behind him and wrapped itself around his mouth.

2

As he scanned the auction room, Nigel Winterford was surprised to find that he was on edge. An auctioneer at London's most famous auction house, he had presided over thousands of sales in his career. The auction room was his court, and he was its impassive, gavel-wielding judge. From up on his podium, Nigel had calmly organized the sale of the most expensive painting ever – an early work by van Gogh, purchased by an Arab sheikh for tens of millions of pounds. When two American businessmen had come to blows over a Rodin sculpture, he had barely batted an eyelid. He had sold priceless works of art to sharp-eyed collectors, and small keepsakes to elderly ladies.

Tonight, though, was something else entirely.

All the lots in this sale had come from the estate of Sir Basil Gresham, a rich philanthropist whose recent death had been greatly mourned. Given Sir Basil's reputation as a connoisseur of antiques, Nigel had been delighted to be chosen to conduct the auction. But, as he began to read the strict sale conditions that came with the items, his misgivings began to grow.

First, the auction was to be conducted at midnight, with only those specifically invited being allowed to attend. No members of the public were permitted entrance. Secondly, the bidding was to be conducted in pre-decimal coinage: guineas and shillings rather than pounds and pence. If this wasn't difficult enough, Nigel had to conduct the auction alone. Normally he would have assistants displaying the lots and taking bids on the telephone from those who couldn't be there in person. But tonight there was only one telephone next to him on the podium – an antiquated model with a handlebar receiver that wouldn't have looked out of place in the sale itself.

Most unsettling of all, Sir Basil's will had stipulated that under no circumstances could the auction be halted. If for any reason Nigel stopped, then all the goods would be withdrawn – losing the auction house a great deal of face, not to mention the chance of a fat commission from the sale of Sir Basil's other works of art.

Having not received a single reply to his invitations, Nigel was somewhat relieved when the first person slinked in through the double doors: an elderly man with bloodshot eyes. The man looked around, nodding at the deep red walls of the auction room with something like approval, before squeezing himself into a chair at the back row.

As the minute hand ticked closer to midnight, the room began to fill with people. Nigel had to confess that he had hoped for a rather more upmarket crowd. These people limped and hobbled, mumbling and cackling, wild eyes bulging out of scarred faces. Their clothes were old-fashioned: dark suits matched with cravats and waistcoats for the men, and flowing, ankle-length dresses for the women. Nigel wondered if they were from some sort of historical society. If that was the case, it was a particularly down-at-heel society. The air rang with shouts and squabbles, while the characteristic smell of lush carpet and wood polish had taken on a sourer aspect, as if a pot-pourri bowl had been doused in vinegar.

Above the hubbub of the crowd, Nigel could just make out the sound of a grandfather clock doling out twelve long strokes. Midnight. Time to begin. He adjusted his bowtie and cleared his throat, just as he had done a thousand times before. This was his job, he reminded himself sternly as he took to the podium. No matter how rough the crowd, he had an auction to conduct.

"Ladies and gentlemen," Nigel began, but even with the aid of a microphone, no one could hear his polite introduction over the din. Two haggard women were bickering loudly in the front row, jabbing accusatory fingers at one another.

"LADIES AND GENTLEMEN!"

The room fell into a shocked silence at the auctioneer's bellow. Even the women in the front row stopped fighting and looked up at the podium.

"Thank you," Nigel continued in a softer voice, smiling

now. "My name is Nigel Winterford and I am pleased to say that I am your auctioneer for this . . . *unique* sale. We shall be displaying items from the collection of Sir Basil Gresham, a man whose reputation for canny and tasteful acquisitions of artwork and jewellery is eclipsed only by his charitable deeds for the Gresham Foundation."

He paused, expecting a response from the audience – a few smiles and nods of recognition, perhaps a spontaneous round of applause. Instead, the temperature of the room seemed to drop several degrees.

"Well, seeing as this event has drawn such a . . . *special* crowd, let's make sure everyone is familiar with auction procedure. You should all have been given a paddle with a number on it." Noting the shrugs and scrabbling under seats that this remark elicited, Nigel decided to plough on regardless. "When you wish to bid for an item, simply raise this paddle. I'll let you know I've seen your bid. Don't worry – you can't bid for anything by mistake. But you've only got yourself to blame if your purchase is too big for the mantelpiece!"

Silence.

"Right then, shall we start? Lot number 1. . ."

It didn't take long for Nigel to realize that this particular auction was not going to go smoothly. The lots were haphazard: antique pistols; hand-carved chairs; rusting thumbscrews; painting after painting of purely black canvases. Very few of the audience seemed interested in actually bidding, preferring to pick fights amongst themselves.

Most of those who did try to bid had lost their paddles, and made their interest known by waving their hands in the air, shouting at the top of their lungs, "Mine!", or – in the worst case – pelting rotten fruit at Nigel. Ordinarily, the auctioneer would have halted the sale immediately, but there was no way he was going to let this rabble cost him his commission. So Nigel took off his bow tie and jacket, rolled up his sleeves and got on with the job.

After selling a series of grotesque gargoyle carvings to the old man in the back row for twenty-five shillings, Nigel was surprised by the feeling of elation that ran through him. Had anyone tried to conduct a sale in such anarchy before? Feeling buoyant, he turned back to the catalogue listing the items for sale.

"Lot 65. An Edwin Spine painting entitled *The Light of Shame*. Shall we start the bidding at tenpence? Sixpence? There's no reserve price on this item, ladies and gentlemen, which means it can go for one penny if needs be. Come on, there must be a bid somewhere! No?"

Peering out over the crowd, Nigel couldn't detect a single intentional bid amongst the flailing arms. Removing the unwanted painting, he turned his attention to the next item: a heavy casket wrought from black steel. He lifted it carefully on to the table next to him before turning back to his catalogue.

"Right, then . . . on to tonight's final item. Lot 66."

The room plunged into a deep, anticipatory silence. Fists unclenched; tussles ceased. Everyone sat down, eyes now firmly fixed on the front of the room. Nigel looked up from the podium. He smiled.

"I see this is an item of some interest to you. Let me read out the description from the catalogue:

> *"The Crimson Stone is the most celebrated of enigmas. Little can be said with any certainty. Its origins are a mystery; its age has never been ascertained. It remains locked away in this presentation case, to ensure that only its rightful owner may gaze upon it. For thirty years it has remained hidden from the outside world, leading some to doubt its very existence. Now, for the first time in a generation, you have the opportunity to claim it for your own.*
>
> *"Popular belief has it that the Crimson Stone was stained with the blood of Jack the Ripper himself, conferring great powers upon both the Stone and those lucky enough to possess it. Whether this is true or not, the Crimson Stone remains an item of incomparable fascination, thought by many to be priceless. We have suggested an opening price of ten-thousand guineas."*

As he spoke, Nigel was delighted to see the audience lean forward, hanging on his every word. At the mention of the price, there was a collective gasp. Whatever this mysterious piece was, it was worth more than the rest of the collection combined, and then some. He was in control now, all right.

"Well then, can I hear an opening bid?"

"Fifteen-thousand guineas!" came a cry from the left side of the room. The bidder was standing by the wall, wrapped up in a cowled red robe, and Nigel couldn't be sure if it was a man or a woman. He did notice, however, that the room swivelled as one to stare at the figure, and that none of the glances were friendly.

"I have fifteen-thousand in the room. Do I hear twenty?"

A girl with flaming red hair shyly lifted her paddle aloft. Despite his professionalism, Nigel did a double take. Where would such a young woman acquire that sort of wealth? Then again, what else about this night was ordinary?

"Twenty from the young lady. Do I hear twenty-five?"

A man stood up from his seat. In all the chaos, Nigel had failed to notice him, which was extraordinary, given his height. He had to be nearly seven feet tall. Without a word, the giant slowly raised his left hand.

"The gentleman bids twenty-five. Do I hear thirty?"

Nigel's pulse was racing now. The cowled figure made a noise of disgust and stalked out of the room. The redheaded girl lifted her paddle again, awkward in the spotlight of malevolent glares.

"Thirty bid. Do I have forty?"

All eyes were on the giant now. It was down to the two of them. The man raised his hand again.

"Forty!" Nigel cried out. "We have forty. Do I hear fifty, miss?"

The girl looked down, seemingly unwilling to bid again.

Then, after what seemed like an eternity, she nodded. There were more gasps, and several loud oaths. Though Nigel could tell that the mood in the room was one of ugly resentment, he was getting carried away by the thrill of the auction. He turned back to the giant.

"Fifty-thousand guineas bid, sir. Do I hear more? Do I hear fifty-five?"

A look of consternation crossed the man's face. He folded his arms and shook his head.

"Ladies and gentlemen, the bid stands at fifty-thousand guineas. Do we have any fresh bidders? No? Going once at fifty-thousand. . ."

The young girl shrank in her seat under a barrage of hisses and catcalls. Nigel almost felt sorry for her. But there was no way he could stop the auction now.

"Going twice. . ."

Out of the corner of his eye, the auctioneer saw a burly figure crack his knuckles threateningly. The girl looked terrified. But what could he do? No one had *forced* her to bid for the item. He raised his gavel.

And then the phone rang.

Nigel nearly dropped the hammer with surprise. The murmuring ceased, leaving the polite but insistent ring as the only sound in the room. The auctioneer lifted the receiver gingerly, as if it were a bomb.

"Hello?" he croaked.

"Mr Winterford?" said a desiccated voice. "My name is Cornelius Xavier. Forgive my absence from the auction. I prefer the comforts of my home to the outside world. What does the bidding stand at?"

"Fifty-thousand guineas, sir."

There was a sharp intake of breath down the phone line.

"My my, that is a lot of money, isn't it? But then, nothing worthwhile ever comes cheaply, Mr Winterford. You may expect my associates presently."

The voice then named his bid, and promptly hung up. When Nigel put the receiver down, his hands were shaking. He returned to the podium and whispered into the microphone.

"One-hundred-thousand guineas."

The room exploded into uproar. Pushes and shoves quickly escalated into punches and kicks. Chairs rained down upon the podium. The redheaded girl was surrounded by a coven of furious old crones, only to be rescued – surprisingly – by the giant, who swatted the women out of the way before picking the girl up and carrying her from the room. They had the right idea, Nigel thought. As he fled towards the safety of a side room, the auctioneer saw a gang of huge men in suits stride into the room and fight their way through the scrum towards the casket on the table. It appeared that Cornelius Xavier's associates had arrived.

Compared to the anarchy in the auction room, the side room was a dingy paradise. Nigel locked the door and leant against it, his heart thudding, the sounds of rioting echoing in his ears. He had been lucky to get out alive.

"Mr Winterford?"

Someone was standing over by the window. Nigel strained to see through the gloom.

"Yes? Who are you?"

"My name is unimportant. I was employed by Sir Basil to ensure that the rules of his will were adhered to."

Nigel drew himself up to his full height.

"As you can see, sir, I have followed every instruction to the last letter, in the most testing of conditions."

"Almost," came the amicable reply. "Every instruction but one."

The auctioneer furiously racked his brains. He had gone over the instructions with a fine-tooth comb. He couldn't have missed anything!

"Oh, don't worry," the voice chuckled. "You've done everything you can. Sir Basil would be delighted. But there was one final instruction that you didn't know about."

"Oh? Which was?"

From somewhere in the darkness came the sound of a sword being drawn.

"No Lightside witnesses. Sir Basil was very particular on that point."

"What? I don't understand!"

The figure took a pace towards Nigel, who stumbled backwards, crashing into a marble sculpture.

"Going. . ."

"Please!" the auctioneer cried. "I beg you!"

"Going. . ."

"This is madness! You wouldn't. . ."

The last thing Nigel Winterford saw was a long blade arcing through the darkness. There was a loud thump as he crashed to the floor.

"Gone," said the voice, contentedly.

3

Jonathan squirmed frantically, but his assailant had him in a tight, muscular grip, a meaty hand staunching his cries for help. He was dragged backwards into a shadowy recess of the car park, his feet scrabbling on the tarmac. Powerless to resist, Jonathan was preparing for the worst when a familiar voice asked: "What *are* you up to, boy?"

Jonathan spun round. Carnegie had relinquished his hold and was now eyeing him with quizzical amusement. The wereman had forsaken his beloved stovepipe hat for a wide-brimmed fedora, but that was his only concession to the modern world. Beneath a long coat he was wearing an old-fashioned three-piece suit, his purple waistcoat splattered and smudged like an artist's palette.

"Jesus, Carnegie!" Jonathan exclaimed, half angrily, half with relief. "You scared the life out of me! What are you doing?"

"I asked first."

"Lightside stuff," he replied defensively. "You wouldn't understand."

"I recognize trouble when I see it."

"Yeah, well, things have been a bit slow round here. I've had to make my own amusement."

Jonathan stared defiantly at Carnegie, who suddenly barked with laughter and patted him on the shoulder, nearly knocking Jonathan over.

"I've missed you too, boy. Shall we get out of here before those goons decide to start looking for you again?"

Jonathan nodded, and made for the car park exit. Though he was pleased to see Carnegie, he couldn't help still feeling sore about the way he had been sent back to Lightside. It was strange having the wereman here with him now, skirting between massed ranks of cars instead of dodging rumbling carriages. He looked up at Carnegie.

"How did you find me? No one knew I was coming here."

"I'm a private detective. That sort of thing is my speciality. And I know your scent so well I could follow it through a manure factory."

"Are you saying I smell?"

Carnegie snorted. "Everyone smells."

They came out on to a bustling main road. Though it was getting late in the afternoon, the sun was still hammering down on to the wide pavements. Thirsty shoppers had laid down their bags and were refreshing themselves at tables outside cafés and bars. In the bright sunshine, the scene looked more like a Mediterranean port than North London. At the bus stop, a group of unruly schoolchildren were arguing loudly with one another. Carnegie wrinkled his nose as he stared at the throng of people.

"Give me the Grand any day. Lightsiders are just so . . . pleased with themselves."

"You get used to it," Jonathan replied sourly. He stopped on the pavement, bustling humanity flowing around him. Then, in a quieter voice, he asked: "Why are you here, Carnegie? Have you found something out? Are we going back to Darkside?"

The wereman glanced at him.

"Not sure yet. Maybe. It depends on what Alain says."

"What's Dad got to do with it?"

"Take me to meet him, and you'll find out. Which way is home?"

Jonathan pointed down the street, where a red double-decker bus was pulling up at the stop. The schoolchildren stopped arguing long enough to get onboard and scramble up to the top deck.

"That way."

Carnegie sighed, and pulled his hat down lower over his head.

"I was worried you might say that. Come on, then."

The two of them headed quickly for the bus. Whereas Jonathan preferred to dodge in and out of the crowds, Carnegie simply barged his way through them, oblivious to the indignant cries of protest. Though he may not have enjoyed being on Lightside, the wereman certainly wasn't scared by it either.

Jonathan scampered aboard the bus just before the door closed and bought a ticket for himself and Carnegie. The downstairs of the bus was crammed with pensioners and pushchairs, so he headed upstairs to the sunlit top deck. Years of travelling on public transport had left Jonathan at ease with the swaying motion of a moving bus, but as Carnegie laboured along the aisle behind him it became clear that the wereman was less than comfortable. The bus began moving, and he clung grimly to the poles as he edged forward. There was a look in his eyes that suggested he would welcome the opportunity to punish someone – in all probability, Jonathan.

There was a spare seat just in front of the bickering schoolchildren. Jonathan smiled as Carnegie slumped gratefully down.

"You all right?"

The wereman nodded stiffly.

"It's the height that gets me," he said. "Give me a carriage any day."

Jonathan pointed out of the window.

"Yeah, but there's a lovely view up here," he said, with mock innocence.

Carnegie muttered an oath under his breath, and looked away.

The bus made slow, staccato progress, struggling through

the late afternoon traffic and halting every couple of minutes to take on more passengers. Immediately behind Jonathan and Carnegie, the gang of schoolchildren were getting more and more boisterous. As the bus stopped yet again, two of them began wrestling. One of them knocked into the back of Carnegie, sending his hat flying to the floor. The wereman whirled round, and fixed the offender with a dangerous stare.

"Yeah, what?" said the kid. "You got a problem, weirdo?"

Carnegie's eyes glinted. Baring his teeth, he lunged forward, firing off a round of rabid, guttural barks. The boy cried out in shock and threw himself out of the way. Jonathan tried to restrain Carnegie, but it was like trying to hold back an avalanche. The wereman lunged forward again, jaws snapping, saliva spraying everywhere, sending the boy crashing to the floor of the bus. Terrified, the gang of schoolchildren ran pell-mell along the aisle and down the steps before clattering off the bus.

The top deck fell into a shocked silence. Carnegie went to retrieve his hat, carefully dusting it off.

"Kids!" he said to himself, almost fondly.

"You can't get away with that here!" hissed Jonathan. "You'll get us arrested!"

"For what? Barking? Leave the thinking to me, boy. You just enjoy your view."

Having suffered from years of neglect, the fact that the Starling house was still standing was a testimony to the enduring nature of Victorian construction. The crumbling brickwork stubbornly refused to give way, still propping up the sagging roof. Battered guttering clung to the side of the building. The windows maintained their grimy lookout. Over the years Jonathan had felt a strange affinity with the house, as if his dad's illness and obsessions had left them both to fend for themselves. He was proud of the fact that they were still standing, the pair of them, bruised but not beaten.

So as he reached home it was a surprise to see that someone had tried to tame the tangled jungle of the front garden: the long grass had been mown, the weeds dug up, the shrubs cut back. A row of black rubbish sacks lined the driveway.

"Someone's been busy," he said thoughtfully.

Carnegie looked the building up and down.

"Nice place. Got character."

"Yeah. I had a feeling you'd approve. Come on."

Jonathan went through the gate by the side of the house and down the passageway to the back garden, where he could hear the sound of whirring. He was confronted with the sight of Alain Starling pushing a rusty lawnmower across the thick grass, ignoring its snarled complaints. Unusually for him, Jonathan's dad was wearing a pair of shorts and a baggy T-shirt. His arms and legs were white and painfully thin, a reminder of his fragile health.

As he watched, Alain came to a halt and wiped the sweat from his forehead with the back of his arm. He straightened at the sight of the Jonathan and the tall figure loping along behind him.

"Hello, son. Seems you've brought a guest."

Carnegie nodded at Jonathan's father.

"Alain."

"Elias," responded Alain.

Jonathan was suddenly acutely aware of how little he knew about the time the two men had spent together in Darkside, the secrets they must have shared. The absence of the person who had brought them together could be felt so keenly that it was almost as if Theresa Starling was standing amongst them. But there was more here, a tension that Jonathan couldn't explain. Why weren't they happier to see each other?

"It's good to see you," Alain said softly. "It's been too long."

Carnegie eyed him critically. "You've been living here for too long. You're getting soft."

"Physically or emotionally?"

"Both."

There was a pause.

"I tried to go back," came the quiet reply.

"I know. You're almost as crazy as the boy."

For a second, all that could be heard in the garden was the lazy droning of insects and a plane passing overhead far above them, before Alain laughed, and the tension melted away.

"Like father, like son, they say. Don't know about you,

but I'm gasping for a drink. Let's go inside."

Clapping Carnegie on the back, Alain led them inside the house. As Jonathan followed on, he was disturbed to see that the wereman wasn't smiling, and his face was grim.

4

Alain rummaged through the fridge and dug out a can of beer.

"Do you want one, Elias?" he called back over his shoulder. "I think there's another cold one in here somewhere. . ."

Carnegie shook his head, and lowered himself rather warily on to a plastic kitchen seat.

"Don't worry about it. I've brought my own."

He reached into his suit pocket and pulled out a dirty brown bottle. The wereman removed the cork, and immediately the pungent odour of his explosive "Special Recipe" flooded the Starlings' kitchen.

"Do you want a Coke, Jonathan?" Alain called out. "Or a lemonade or something?"

"I'm fine, Dad. Come and sit down."

His dad was acting odd, trying too hard to play the perfect host. He was clearly nervous, though Jonathan couldn't imagine why. Was it simply because he hadn't seen

Carnegie for years, or was there another, more complicated reason?

Alain settled into a chair and popped open the ringpull on his can. Tipping his head back, he took a long, thirsty gulp.

"So then," he said, wiping his mouth. "What brings you to Lightside, Elias?"

"I was missing the boy," Carnegie replied grumpily. "It's been weeks since anyone tried to kill me."

Alain laughed. "I hope he wasn't too much bother."

"Nearly as bad for my health as you were. Your whole damn family should come with a warning."

A serious look replaced the smile on Alain's face.

"I don't know what might have happened had you not taken care of him," he said quietly. "I am indebted to you, Elias."

"Not a problem. Though you might want to think before making too many promises like that. The boy ran up quite a large debt in a short time."

"Hey! I am here, you know," Jonathan said peevishly. He hated the way adults always talked about children as if they weren't there. Alain ruffled his hair fondly, irritating Jonathan even more, then turned back to the wereman.

"But seriously, Elias, why did you come over to Lightside? I know the atmosphere doesn't agree with you. Is it something to do with Theresa?"

Carnegie took a swig from the dirty bottle, wincing as the fiery liquid scalded his throat. Then he nodded.

"It might be nothing, but I heard something I thought was worth checking with you."

Jonathan leant forward expectantly.

"I was playing cards at the Casino Sanguino and found myself up against a wight called Ismael. You ever met a wight?"

Jonathan shook his head.

"Foul creatures – sneaky and underhand. Anyway, Ismael was not having the luckiest night, and before too long he owed me a pile of shillings. But I made the mistake of leaving him alone with the dealer for a minute, and when I returned to the table he was nowhere to be seen. Obviously, I couldn't let him get away with that. If word gets around Darkside you can't collect your debts, people'll lose all respect for you.

"I found out that Ismael had gone into hiding on Robbers' Marsh, and after several nights scouring the area I managed to track down his barrow. It's fair to say that Ismael was not exactly happy to see me, especially when I started hitting him. He told me he didn't have any money and started begging for mercy. When that didn't work, he offered to give me some information. So I stopped hitting him and waited to see if he knew anything useful."

"And?" asked Alain.

The wereman scratched his cheek.

"It was all fairly incoherent. I think he would have confessed to murdering James Ripper if he thought it would have helped. But then he mentioned the Cain Club, and my ears pricked up. So I shook him around some more and he told me that he had overheard a conversation about a guy called Orcus, who had made a fortune organizing the kidnapping of a female reporter who had been asking awkward questions. Now, I'm not in the habit of trusting wights, but it sounded pretty familiar to my ears. I've put the word out but I can't find anyone who's heard of this guy Orcus. Does the name mean anything to you? Did Theresa ever say anything about him?"

Alain rested his head in his hands, concentrating hard. Eventually he looked up and shook his head.

"If she did, it's not something she ever mentioned to me. Though," he added wryly, "it wouldn't be the only thing she wasn't telling me. She never said a word about the Cain Club at the time."

"Like I said," Carnegie replied, "it may be nothing. I just figured it was worth asking."

"Maybe Mrs Elwood might know something," Jonathan piped up. "They used to know each other, didn't they?"

The wereman looked blank.

"Who?"

"Of course!" replied Alain. "You've never met Lily Elwood, have you? She's a Darksider too. She crossed over after Theresa went missing. She's a wonderful woman – I don't think Jonathan and I could have got by without her. Why don't we go and say hello now? She only lives a couple of houses down the road."

He finished off his beer and rose from the table. With a sigh, Carnegie tucked his bottle back into his suit pocket.

Compared to the battered Starling residence, Mrs Elwood's house was a picture of ordered calm. Jonathan could see its neatly trimmed lawn from his bedroom window, a sight he had always found reassuring. He had stayed there a few times when his dad had been in hospital, and it had been an oasis of sanity during troubled times. Just walking up the driveway made him more relaxed. This time, however, he saw immediately that something was wrong. Jonathan stopped suddenly and clutched Carnegie's arm.

"What's up, boy?"

"The side gate's open. Ever since she got burgled a couple of years back she's kept it locked all the time – even when she's in. I left it open once and she went absolutely mental."

"Maybe she just forgot this time."

A grim look passed over Alain's face.

"Lily never forgets. He's right – there's something wrong."

Carnegie tipped his hat back on his forehead and stretched his grizzled neck muscles, as if he was preparing for a fight. There was a loud click as something popped back into place.

"You two stay here," the wereman growled. "I'll let you know when you can come in."

He stalked on up the driveway, his coat trailing out behind him. Pausing at the window to peer inside, he tried the front door handle. The door swung smoothly open. The wereman glanced back at Jonathan and Alain, and then moved inside, closing the door silently behind him.

"Don't worry, son," said Alain, noting the look of concern on Jonathan's face. "If there's anything wrong, Elias'll sort it out."

Jonathan said nothing, tapping his foot with impatience. He wasn't used to waiting outside. A minute passed by with agonizing slowness, then another. What was taking Carnegie so long?

"I can't stand this," he said eventually. "I'm going in."

"Jonathan! Wait!"

It was too late. He had already marched off, and within seconds had slipped through the front door and followed the wereman into the house.

He padded around the ground floor, his footsteps sounding deafening in the silence. Jonathan had been dreading the signs of a violent struggle, but everything was where he remembered it: the fruit bowl on the kitchen table, the arrangement of yellow flowers in the front room, the notepad and pencil placed carefully next to the phone in the hallway. But despite the fact that nothing had been disturbed, Jonathan couldn't shake the feeling that something bad had happened. Where was Carnegie?

He climbed the staircase and found the wereman standing in the bedroom, looking thoughtfully at a piece of paper. An envelope was lying on the bed. He looked up as Jonathan entered.

"What happened to waiting outside?" he growled.

"There was a change of plan. What's going on? Where is she?"

"No idea. I've been through the entire house and there's no one here. At first I thought she'd just gone out, but then I saw this. The envelope was addressed to you."

He passed the paper to Jonathan. A note had been scrawled on it in simple, childlike letters:

We have the dwarf. Go to London Zoo tomorrow afternoon at exactly four o'clock, and wait for the zebra inside the entrance. Then we will discuss the conditions for her release. Come alone or the dwarf won't see the end of the day. You will be watched.

Jonathan looked up fearfully at the wereman, who gestured at the neatly folded bedspread.

"It's strange. There's no sign of a struggle. If someone did take her, it's one of the smoothest kidnappings I've ever seen. Can we be sure this is for real?"

Jonathan picked up the envelope from the bed and, his hands suddenly trembling, pulled out several strands of Mrs Elwood's long, blonde hair.

"This is real, all right."

5

A storm was in the offing. Jonathan hurried down Prince Albert Road under a blanket of swollen grey clouds. The heat had curdled, and the atmosphere was charged with electricity. He could feel beads of sweat dampening his armpits and coating his palms – but whether this was due to the weather conditions or apprehension, Jonathan couldn't be sure.

He didn't want to admit it, but he was nervous. During his time in Darkside, Jonathan had compiled a short but poisonous list of enemies, any one of whom could have organized the kidnapping of Mrs Elwood. He wished that Carnegie was striding alongside him. The wereman had wanted to go with him, but the note had been brutally clear on that point: Jonathan had to go alone. Even if Lucien Ripper was lying in wait for him, Jonathan couldn't risk any harm coming to Mrs Elwood. In Theresa's absence, she had been the closest thing to a mum he had known. The thought of losing her as well was unbearable.

Nestling in the grounds of Regent's Park, London Zoo had the air of a secret world all of its own. Skirting round the outside of the genteel park, it was hard to imagine the big cats and gorillas that were roaming around within. Through the first few spits of rain, Jonathan spotted the entrance on the Outer Circle road. It was late afternoon, not long before the zoo closed, and there was no queue at the front gates. Jonathan paid his entrance fee, clattered through the turnstile and surveyed his surroundings.

At first glance, there wasn't much to see. A network of paths snaked gently down the slope, before disappearing off behind the different enclosures. Only the distant squawk of small birds and the thick smell of dung gave any clue that there were animals present at all. The lateness of the day and the approaching storm had kept the crowds away, and there were only a handful of people milling around near the entrance. Defying the weather, a family tucked into ice creams outside the café, while a group of foreign tourists laughingly compared photographs on their mobile phones. Outside the staked walls of the Gorilla Kingdom, a crocodile of primary school children in brightly coloured jumpers were shouting and squealing with delight.

The rain began to beat a more insistent rhythm on the ground. Jonathan checked his watch anxiously. It was five past four. The zebra should have been here by now, but there was no sign of one, and there was no mention of a zebra enclosure on the map. And anyway, he couldn't imagine animals were allowed to wander freely around the zoo. It didn't make any sense. Was the note in code? What if there had already been a sign and he had missed it? Would they hurt Mrs Elwood?

More tourists were trudging into view, huddling together against the slanting rain as they made their way back towards the turnstiles. A high-pitched scream made Jonathan whirl round, but it was only one of the school children refusing to put on a plastic anorak. He was about to turn away when there was a movement above the sea of heads. Wiping the damp hair from his eyes, Jonathan saw an umbrella opening out slowly into the air. It had black and white vertical stripes, like an animal's markings. The zebra! Whoever was holding the umbrella was standing with their back to Jonathan, their figure obscured behind a long brown coat, and as he watched they walked away down the left path. There was nothing else to do but follow them.

The figure headed north, against the tide of the crowds washing towards the exit. Jonathan stayed several paces behind, unsure of whether he wanted to catch up with them, or whether he was scared of discovering their identity. They moved on, down through the underpass that ran under the Outer Circle, two sets of footsteps echoing off the walls, and out into the second, smaller part of the zoo. It was deserted, and Jonathan's heartbeat raced as he turned right and followed along the pathway towards a small building. At the entrance to the building, the figure took down its umbrella and turned around.

"Hello, Jonathan," said Marianne Ripper.

And really, he should have known that it would be her. Darkside's finest bounty hunter had somehow acquired a zookeeper's outfit, and was wearing a safari-style shirt, shorts and Wellington boots. Her hair had been tied back, save for a single lock that tumbled down her cheek – a violent shade of lime green glowing against the backdrop of her pale skin. Jonathan took a deep breath, unwilling to give her the satisfaction of looking shocked.

"Oh. It's you."

"Is that all? You don't look at all pleased to see me. At the very least, I thought you'd be surprised."

"Yeah, well, you're never far away when there's trouble around."

She flashed him a dazzling smile. "What a lovely thing to say!"

As usual, Jonathan couldn't quite decide whether she was mocking him or not, and whether he hated her or not. He tried to ignore the faint aroma of her perfume, which in the past had acted as a powerful sedative. Then the image of Mrs Elwood and the note raced through his mind, and his resolve hardened.

"You've kidnapped one of my friends, Marianne. I want her back."

The bounty hunter sighed with disappointment.

"The older you get, Jonathan, the more serious you become. Before long, you're going to be no fun at all." A half-smile played on Marianne's lips. "Very well, then. Let's go inside. If we must talk business, there's someone you need to say hello to."

She held open the door to the building, and Jonathan moved reluctantly past her. Inside the air was artificially hot and humid, and faint wafts of steam rose from Jonathan's soaked clothing. Marianne led him past a "Creatures of the Rainforest" exhibition, and down a flight of steps in the middle of the room. As he went, Jonathan saw the sign "Night Zone", and with a sickening lurch he realized who was waiting in the darkness below. His instinctive reaction was to turn on his heels and flee, but a hand darted out and fastened on to his wrist like a vice.

"He'll only get angry if you keep him waiting," Marianne hissed softly into his ear. "And if you do care about your friend, you *really* don't want that."

He had no choice. His shoulders sagging, Jonathan allowed the bounty hunter to lead him on down the stairs.

The Night Zone was a gloomy haven for the nocturnal creatures, hiding them from the piercing glare of the sun. It was a dark world of shuffling and scuttling; of tiny faces dominated by huge, saucer-shaped eyes. As Marianne took him deeper into the bowels of the exhibit, Jonathan could see that something was terribly wrong. The jumping rats cowered in the corner of their casement, the scorpions sheltered under rocks, while the poisonous frogs trembled underwater. Like him, they could sense the presence of a powerful predator.

In the main room two people had gathered in front of a

glass panel. A tall, elegant man with fair hair stood alongside a redheaded girl clad in a long black dress: the vampire Vendetta, and his maidservant Raquella. Behind the glass panel, a cortège of fruit bats were chirruping excitedly at the onlookers. They clambered around the branches like monkeys, their claws glinting, before unfurling their wings and exploding into flight.

"Guess who I found wandering around the zoo?" Marianne called out.

Vendetta didn't turn around. Raquella cast a grave glance over her shoulder.

"That's right! Jonathan Starling! I thought you'd be pleased."

She dragged the boy over to stand beside the vampire, who was transfixed by the fruit bats.

"Do you know," he began finally, in a conversational tone, "exactly how many ways I could kill your friend?"

"Mrs Elwood's done nothing to you!" Jonathan cried, wriggling to break free from Marianne's grip. "It's me you want! You leave her alone!"

Vendetta gave a ghastly chuckle. "Don't worry. She's safe for now. Whether she remains that way depends entirely upon you."

"What do you want?" Jonathan said, through gritted teeth.

The vampire gestured curtly to Raquella. "Give him the cutting."

The maidservant handed him a front page from *The Darkside Informer*, which was dominated by a single article:

CRIMSON STONE FOUND!

By Arthur Blake

For a few sensational, precious minutes last night, the Crimson Stone was back in the public eye – only for it to disappear as quickly as it had arrived. Reputed to contain the very essence of Darkside, and convey great power to its owner, the Stone's history has been shrouded in mystery. Apparently treasured by Jack Ripper, it disappeared during the reign of his son Albert. In recent years, some Darkside scholars have even claimed that the Stone was a myth designed to tighten the Ripper's grip on power – erroneously, it seems.

The Stone came to light during a special auction of Basil Gresham's possessions. "Basil the Burglar" was one of the most talented thieves of his day, until he decided to make a new life for himself in Lightside. It now appears that he took the Crimson Stone with him. Following frenetic bidding driven by representatives of Darkside notables G. Vendetta and Marianne Ripper, the Stone was claimed by a group of men this reporter can confirm work for Cornelius Xavier, the immensely wealthy Darkside silk merchant, who himself now lives in Lightside. Mr Xavier was unavailable for comment.

Wealthy recluse wins bidding for coveted Darkside treasure

Jonathan's brow wrinkled with confusion.

"OK," he said slowly. "And?"

The vampire didn't move, his eyes fixed on the chirruping creatures in front of him.

"You'll notice that both Marianne and myself were thwarted in our attempts to acquire this precious stone. Xavier's intervention was entirely unexpected. He's been hidden away in his Lightside mansion for years – there were rumours that he had gone insane. However, it seems he is very much alive and well. Now Marianne and I have joined forces to wrest the Crimson Stone from his withered old hands."

"What does this have to do with me?"

Marianne gave him a sweet smile.

"Don't you see? *You're* going to get the Stone for us, Jonathan!"

"What? How?"

"I don't know – ask nicely?"

"You have a week," the vampire coldly intoned. "Produce the Stone by midnight next Thursday or your beloved Mrs Elwood will be introduced to the notion of pain."

"But this is impossible!" Jonathan protested. "I'm not a thief!"

"Well, for Mrs Elwood's sake, I sincerely hope you learn. And quickly. At least you've got your pet mongrel for help. He always seems to have an answer for everything."

Jonathan stopped in his tracks. "But . . . how do you know Carnegie is here?"

Marianne broke into a silvery peal of laughter. "Oh, Jonathan. You can be enchantingly naïve sometimes. Dear old Elias is here because we sent him." She turned to Vendetta. "What did you tell Ismael to say to him again?"

The vampire waved an airy hand. "Some nonsense about his mother. I left the exact details up to the wight. Whatever Ismael said, it sent the mangy cur scurrying over here at top speed."

"What?" Jonathan said fiercely. "You lied about my mum?"

"You should be thankful he did," Marianne cut in. "Would you rather do this on your own?" The bounty hunter traced a nail down his cheek, even as he shied away from her touch. "Jonathan, my father has retired to his bed, and he will not rise from it again. If the Crimson Stone does possess magical powers, I cannot allow it to fall into the wrong hands. You know Lightside better than any of us. I'm counting on you to succeed."

"But . . . I don't even know where this Xavier guy lives!"

"Raquella has his address," replied Vendetta. "She can tell you on the way back."

The maidservant started. "Sir? But. . ."

The vampire gave her a small, cruel smile. "Oh, did I not tell you you're going with him? You always seem so eager to help the boy out – I thought I'd make it easier for you this time and save you the trouble of betraying me again. Am I not a kind and generous master?"

"But, sir, you have only just recovered from your illness! Surely you need someone to attend upon you?"

"I imagine that I'll survive. Go now. And don't bother coming back without the Stone."

Looking slightly dazed, Raquella moved away from her master and stood by Jonathan's side.

"What an adorable couple!" Marianne exclaimed, her voice heavy with mockery.

As the two teenagers trailed forlornly towards the exit of the Night Zone, the bounty hunter shot Vendetta a sideways glance.

"Satisfied?"

The vampire shrugged. "Either we get the Stone, or Starling dies. I can't lose either way."

"I suppose," mused the bounty hunter. "It would be a shame if Jonathan died, though. I do enjoy our little encounters."

"Don't tell me you're growing fond of the boy. Such weakness is highly unbecoming of a Ripper. Or does the fact that you're a woman make you susceptible to moments of such . . . tenderness?"

Marianne arched a single, sculpted eyebrow. "You are welcome to test my mettle any time you wish, vampire."

Vendetta snorted. "I don't think that will be necessary – just yet."

The bounty hunter pushed a lime-green lock behind her ear, her forehead creased in thought. "You know, I have a sneaking suspicion that he'll find a way to get his hands on the Stone. He is a resourceful creature."

"Are you willing to place a wager on that?"

"Of course."

"If the boy dies, you pay me ten guineas. If he retrieves the Stone, I pay you ten guineas."

"And the winner gets to kill Ismael."

Vendetta's fangs flashed in the darkness.

"Really, Marianne, you are quite the brightest treasure on Darkside. Deal."

6

From the moment Jonathan guided a stunned Raquella through the front door of the Starling house, it was clear that Elias Carnegie was in a surly temper. And that was before he had heard about what had taken place at the zoo, and what Vendetta had demanded.

"Blasted vampire! I'll tear him into pieces!" he raged, hurling a glass against the kitchen wall as the rest of the room watched in shocked silence. "No more of his bidding. No more of these bloody games!"

"Elias, calm down!" Alain pleaded.

The wereman leant towards Jonathan, and the boy could sense the beast within Carnegie desperately trying to claw its way to the surface.

"You don't get it, do you, boy?" he whispered. "You think that somehow you'll steal this stone for them and that'll be it. You don't understand. This will never end. They will never leave you alone. The best thing for you – and your friend – is if I go and pay Vendetta and that bounty hunter a visit."

Jonathan stared at Carnegie's wild eyes, heard the raggedness in his voice, and came to a decision.

"No," he said, quietly but decisively. "I've already lost one mum. I'm not going to lose another. After we get Mrs Elwood back you can do what you want, but until then we're going to get this stupid stone, and you're not going to place her in any more danger, OK?"

Carnegie swore and argued until late into the night, but Jonathan refused to be swayed. Realizing that for once he was beaten, the wereman eventually relented.

"All right. I'll come with you. But this is a fool's errand, and you should know it. Both of you."

With a final meaningful glance at Alain, the wereman stomped off upstairs, muttering darkly to himself. Jonathan's dad seemed unmoved, his brow wrinkled.

"What is it, Dad?"

"Might be nothing. It's just that I'm sure I've heard the name Cornelius Xavier before. I might flick through a couple of books before I go to bed, see if I can dig anything up."

"You want a hand?"

Alain shook his head. "You need to get your rest. You've got a mansion to stake out tomorrow."

Cornelius Xavier's residence was located in Kensington, a wealthy borough in the south-west of the capital where multi-million-pound flats and giant mansions hobnobbed with exclusive boutiques and labyrinthine department stores. It was where the international jet set lived, in between their skiing holidays and Caribbean cruises.

The most desired houses were located on an exclusive street called Slavia Avenue – a quiet, tree-lined avenue off Kensington High Street that ran for a quarter of a mile up a gentle incline. Early the next morning, Jonathan and a rather grumpy wereman found themselves surveying the surroundings. A long green stretched out languidly on the right-hand side. On the left, a squadron of giant houses drew themselves stiffly to attention. Foreign embassies proudly displayed their national flags, like medals pinned to a soldier's chest. All the buildings sheltered behind steepling walls and banks of security cameras.

Although members of the public were allowed to walk down Slavia Avenue, they had to pass security booths at each end, and large signs warned that photography was forbidden. Outside one embassy, Jonathan was surprised to see a group of armed policemen cradle guns as they scanned the road.

Amongst all the grand architectural posturing, the Xavier residence was something of an oddity. It was set back from the road, in the shadow of two huge oak trees. All that could be seen of the building, above a towering brick wall bedecked with iron spikes and barbed wire, was the tip of its slanting roof. The only way in or out of the compound appeared to be through a thick metal gate.

"This place is a bloody fortress!" Jonathan exclaimed. "Who *is* this guy Xavier?"

Carnegie frowned. "Beyond his name, I don't know much more than gossip and rumours. He made a fortune running silk factories back in Darkside. By all accounts, they were little more than hellholes – people working twenty hours a day, kids getting mangled in the machinery – and Xavier seemed to relish making the conditions as foul as possible. Even Darksiders tended to give him a wide berth.

"Anyway, he moved over here a few years back, and that's been about it. People say he's paranoid and he's mad and he never leaves the house. Maybe none of it is true – maybe all of it. What I do know is, you don't mess with him lightly."

From somewhere across the green, a bell began tolling nine o'clock. As his head turned to follow the sound, Jonathan noticed a limousine drawing up to the gates of the Xavier residence.

"There's a car pulling up!" he said urgently.

"Do up your shoelaces. And don't hurry."

Jonathan got down on one knee and promptly undid his laces, trying not to appear too conspicuous. Glancing up at the limousine as it swished past, he saw that the windows were tinted black and the bodywork had been armour-plated. When it was within yards of the mansion, the heavy front gates swung open with a sonorous hum. Jonathan caught a glimpse of a gravel driveway and a building with an ugly, gothic façade. Beside him, Carnegie stared openly through the gate.

"What are you doing?" hissed Jonathan. "Bit obvious, isn't it?"

"Not a crime to look at something, boy. If anyone wants to come out and tell me different, they're more than welcome."

The limousine came to a smooth halt in the driveway, and a bodyguard of suited men carrying guns leapt out. Checking the area was secure, they opened a passenger door and helped Cornelius Xavier out of the car. The Darkside silk merchant was one of the oddest-looking men Jonathan had ever seen in his life. A little over five feet tall, he had a painfully crooked posture. A voluminous robe covered in white symbols couldn't fail to disguise a bulbous belly, nor could a giant pair of dark glasses mask his sagging, aged skin. He shuffled across the gravel in an uneven gait that made him look even older.

As Xavier made for the mansion, one of his bodyguards tripped up on the pathway and stumbled into him. The silk merchant gave the unfortunate man a withering look and then, without warning, struck him across the back of the head with his cane. The bodyguard fell to the floor, poleaxed. Xavier was over him with surprising speed, landing blow after blow on the prone body as the rest of his retinue looked on impassively. Eventually satisfied with the beating, he straightened up and tossed the bloodied cane to another bodyguard, catching sight of Jonathan and Carnegie as he did so. Xavier gave them both a long, cold stare that seemed to penetrate his dark glasses before the gate swung shut, once again cutting off his fortress from the outside world.

"Jesus," Jonathan whistled, as they hurried away, "that was horrible. Did you see how quickly he moved?"

"Pretty nimble for a pensioner," Carnegie agreed. "Something's not right about this. I don't like it one bit."

He cleared his throat and spat a dirty gob of phlegm into the gutter. "So let's recap what we've learnt. Strong perimeter security. Cameras everywhere. Armed guards. And that's just outside. Inside, you've got that psychopath wandering around – who I doubt is going to take too kindly to us trying to walk off with his prize valuable. It's a suicide mission."

Despite the peerlessly blue sky and the sun warming his back, Jonathan felt cold.

"But we'll think of a way to get round that, won't we?" he asked hopefully.

Carnegie fixed Jonathan with a long stare. "Boy, I know we've been through some scrapes together, but you've got to realize there's no way you and I can get in and out of that mansion alive."

"But then Vendetta will kill Mrs Elwood! Whatever it takes, we've got to get the Stone!"

"I know," the wereman replied slowly. "I just don't think we're going to be able to do this on our own. We're going to need help. Professional help."

"What, you mean thieves?"

Carnegie's eyes narrowed. "No, boy, chefs. We'll bake our way inside. Of course I mean thieves."

"But . . . how? Where will we find them?"

The wereman grimaced. "If you want to find jewel thieves, boy, there's only one place to go. And it ain't round here."

Later, under the cover of night, three figures stole through the cobbled streets of Wapping towards the riverfront. Even though the sky was dark, the air was still warm. Muffled up in a thick black cloak, Jonathan wondered for the umpteenth time why on earth Carnegie had insisted that they all wear these garments.

They had returned to the house just long enough to pick up Raquella and receive an absent-minded farewell from Alain Starling. In his quest for information on Cornelius Xavier, Jonathan's dad had re-immersed himself in his study, and was poring over musty books by candlelight. It was a reminder of the bad old days before Jonathan had learnt about Darkside, and as he left the house he felt a twinge of worry.

Judging by the determined set to Raquella's jaw, she had recovered from Vendetta abandoning her at the zoo. She walked briskly by Jonathan's side, the pair of them fighting to keep pace with Carnegie. The maid hadn't said a word throughout the journey, and Jonathan had the distinct impression that somehow she was blaming him for the situation. Suddenly desperate to break the silence, he scrambled around for something to say.

"I can't believe there's another crossing point round

here," he said eventually. "How many of them are there?"

"Too many," Raquella replied coldly, without breaking stride.

"Just, it's not easy crossing, especially if you're pure Darksider. It seems odd there's so many ways you can do it."

"Most Darksiders don't know any – and don't want to know. It's usually only the desperate who learn the location of a crossing point, and the powerful who learn more than one."

"And you, of course," Jonathan said lightly. "You must be an expert on crossing now."

Raquella shot him an icy glare. "Yes, well, if I had been given a choice in the matter, I wouldn't know a single one either. I would be better off without the pain that such journeys cause me. But then some people don't have a choice, Jonathan, do they?"

"Aw, hey, Raq—"

Before he had a chance to finish, Carnegie gestured for silence. The wereman had stopped outside a pub called The Redblood. It was past closing time, and the last patrons had long since staggered off into the night. Now the windows were dark, and the curtains drawn. After a couple of shifty glances up and down the street, Carnegie went prowling along a narrow alleyway that ran alongside the pub, coming to a halt in front of a door set into the side of the building. He knocked softly three times.

There were the sound of footsteps from within, and then a small boy in a tattered shirt and pair of shorts answered the door. He was holding a lamp in one hand and rubbing his eyes with the other.

"Yeah?" he said, his voice thick with sleep. "What d'you want?"

"Good evening, Philip," Carnegie said ominously.

The urchin lifted up his lamp. His eyes bulged when he caught side of the wereman's grizzled face.

"Ripper have mercy! Mr Carnegie! This is a surprise, sir! Been a long time since I saw *you*."

"Not nearly long enough. I trust you and your brother are keeping your noses clean these days?"

"As good as gold these days, sir. On my honour."

The wereman raised an eyebrow. "Whatever that's worth," he replied wryly. "Look, we need passage back to Darkside. Is there a boat free?"

"Always a boat for you, Mr Carnegie. Why don't you come inside?"

The boy pushed the door open, and the wereman strode inside. Raquella gave Jonathan another cold glance.

"After you," he said.

She swept imperiously past him, lifting up the edges of her cloak as if it were a queen's robe. Following her into the gloom, Jonathan felt a shiver of anticipation run down his spine. They were going home.

7

The small Darkside boy led the group along a cramped corridor running along the back of The Redblood, his lantern bobbing like a will o' the wisp. It wasn't long before they came out at the top of a spiralling stone staircase, where the boy came to a halt. Philip raised his lamp, and gave the party a meaningful look.

"All sorts can happen down here. Don't dawdle now, eh?"

Jonathan's pulse quickened. This was what he had been waiting for, what he had been missing so keenly for the past month. His Darkside blood – his mother's blood – stirred from its slumbers at the threat of danger, churning in his veins, urging him onward. The rotten borough was so close he felt he could almost touch it.

They began to descend the staircase, every now and again passing by a door in the outer wall. The steps were treacherously steep, and soon Jonathan's knees were aching. At the head of the party, Philip bounded down like a gazelle, leaving the others so far behind that at times his light threatened to disappear entirely. In the darkness, Jonathan heard a variety of strange noises emanating from behind the doors: a spittle-flecked chorus of a bawdy sea shanty; a woman half-cackling, half-screaming with laughter; and, on the other side of one heavily bolted door, a snuffling and scrabbling noise that made him veer to the opposite side of the staircase.

After what felt like an age, the steps ended and they came out into a low vaulted chamber. Several paces into the room, the floor dropped away, succeeded by a vast expanse of black water that swept on through arch after arch. Peering out over the water, Jonathan could see that large numbers had been daubed in red paint over the arches nearest to them. Down at the water's edge, two long, narrow boats gambolled on the current, pulling at their mooring ropes like dogs on a leash. This far underneath the ground, the air was crisp and cold.

Jonathan let out a low whistle. "This is some cellar," he said. "Do the people who own the pub know about this?"

Philip gave him a scornful look. "I should think so. They built it, after all. They've been ferrying people over for fifty years. Any Darksider who finds himself on this side of town ends up in The Redblood sooner or later." He turned back to the wereman. "So which part of Darkside are you headed for, Mr Carnegie?"

"Slattern Gardens."

"Really, sir?" There was a note of surprise in Philip's

voice. "Been a few years since you've been there, hasn't it? You sure it's a wise idea?"

"Not really," Carnegie replied, vigorously scratching the back of his neck, "but I haven't got much choice."

"If you say so. It's through arch seven, sir."

The wereman gave him a pointed look. "Well, obviously. It's not been *that* long."

Philip went over to the edge of the quay and hopped lightly down into one of the boats, his feet adjusting automatically to the rocking motion. He carried out a quick check underneath the seating before leaping back on to the quay.

"That one there should do you. Worth a shilling of anyone's money, I reckon."

"We'll see."

The wereman flipped him a coin and jumped into the boat, landing with such ease that Jonathan suspected he had spent more time down here than he was letting on. Carnegie turned back and helped Raquella step gracefully down, before extending a hand to Jonathan. Trying to imitate Philip, Jonathan ignored the offer and leapt from the quay. Although he managed to land on two feet, the violent swaying of the boat immediately knocked him off balance. Only Carnegie's outstretched hand saved him from toppling over the side of the craft and into the murky waters beyond.

"Easy does it, boy. You nearly had us all in there."

"Yeah. Sorry."

Trying to hide his embarrassment, Jonathan looked up to see Philip reaching out to hand him the lantern.

"Here, you'd better take the lamp as well. Just in case anything tries to jump out at you."

Jonathan looked nervously at the black water. "Is there anything in there?"

"What . . . like monsters? Nah." Philip looked reflective for a second. "Well, probably not. But better safe than sorry, I always says."

Carnegie looked up from the back of the boat. "Where are the blasted oars? All I can find is this." He held up a long pole.

"That's how you propel this boat, sir. It's a gondola."

"A *what*?" Carnegie's voice was low with menace. "Get me oars, boy."

Philip began to hurriedly untie the mooring rope.

"Don't blame me, Mr Carnegie, sir," he called out. "We're out of rowboats, and we're out of oars. Gondolas and poles is all I've got."

"Don't untie that rope!"

It was too late. Philip unhitched the rope and tossed it to Carnegie as the gondola began to drift away from the quay.

"Arch seven! That way! You'll be through in no time!"

With that, the boy scampered out of the chamber and back up the staircase. Growling with anger, Carnegie clambered to the back of the gondola and jabbed the pole down into the water, bringing the boat to a shuddering standstill.

"How I am meant to steer this dratted thing?" he asked.

"Push the pole off the bottom, and then trail it out in the water behind you," Raquella replied. "Use it like a rudder."

After a couple of minutes of circular splashing, the wereman managed to direct the gondola towards arch number seven. This small success failed to improve his mood.

"When I get my hands on that kid," he muttered, "I'm going to invent new ways to hurt him."

Raquella giggled. "Oh, don't be so gruff. I think you look very dashing."

"Aren't you going to sing us a song while you're up there?" Jonathan added slyly.

"I'd be very careful if I were you," the wereman warned. "If I can't hurt Philip, I may have to settle for you two."

Jonathan laughed and settled back into the gondola. He was coming to the conclusion that this might not be such a bad journey after all when, passing underneath arch seven, he looked up and saw that the number had been painted in thick globules and splatters of a red substance that looked horribly like blood.

The gondola glided on past the arch, and down a long channel. The walls crowded in around them, and when Jonathan held up the lamp, he could see patches of dank mould growing where water lapped up against the brickwork. Beyond the outer reaches of the lamp's orange glow, the darkness was total and unanswerable. The only sounds were the sighing of the current, the splashing of the pole, and Carnegie's grunts of exertion as he propelled the boat forward.

Jonathan's unease was complicated by the fact that they were nearing the Darkside boundary. His stomach was trampolining, and a vein in his forehead was throbbing painfully. It wouldn't be long now before they crossed. Searching for a distraction, he looked across at Raquella.

"Where did Carnegie say we were going again? Some sort of garden?"

"Slattern Gardens," she replied. "It's where all the jewel traders work. If you want to buy or sell a gem in Darkside, it's the only place to go."

"But we want jewel thieves, not jewellers!"

"And where do you think the jewellers get their wares from?" Carnegie's voice cut through the darkness from the gondola's stern. "Do you think their customers find diamonds in the street? You've been on Lightside for too long. Believe me, boy, if anyone can lead us to a jewel thief, it's the ladies of Slattern Gardens."

"Ladies?"

Raquella sighed as Jonathan gave her a quizzical look. "Honestly, I wish there was some sort of guide to Darkside we could give you. Only women are allowed into Slattern Gardens. They sell the jewels, they buy the jewels. The Gardens are ruled by the Queenpin, whose job it is to ensure that no men enter."

"So how are we going to get in?"

"Why do you think we're wearing these ridiculous cloaks?" answered Carnegie.

Jonathan held up his lamp and eyed the tall wereman.

"You make one odd-looking woman. Are you trying to tell me you've got into this place dressed like this before?"

The wereman coughed uncomfortably. "Once or twice. Believe me when I say, boy, there are odder-looking women out there. You'll learn that when you're older. Now hush, and put your hood up. We're nearly there. And for pity's sake, let Raquella do the talking."

Bright lights were burning up ahead, and the sound of chattering voices carried along the widening channel. The gondola emerged from the darkness into a brightly lit cavern. Seams of ores and minerals glittered in the rocks like constellations. On one side of the cavern, a flotilla of boats was tied up beside a wooden jetty. Carnegie carefully navigated the gondola through the river traffic and tethered it up against a small rowing boat.

A figure was standing guard at the edge of the jetty, dressed in a flowing maroon robe. As Jonathan climbed out of the gondola, he was surprised to see that it was a young girl, maybe eleven or twelve years old. Even more eye-catching was the wickedly curved knife tucked into her belt.

"What is your business here?" she asked curtly.

"Why, to trade gems," Raquella replied meekly. "Just like everyone else."

The girl looked them up and down suspiciously. "Why the matching outfits?"

"My sisters and I are in mourning," Raquella replied. "Our beloved father passed away several days ago, leaving us a meagre number of gems with which to secure our future. We have come to the Gardens to see what money we can raise by selling them."

"Really?" The girl drew her knife, and tapped the flat of her blade against the maid's cheek. "I'm not sure I believe you. Why don't you show me these meagre gems?"

Raquella took down her hood, sending her flaming hair tumbling down her back. The girl stepped back in shock.

"You recognize me?" Raquella hissed, through clenched teeth. "You know of my master?"

The girl nodded frantically.

"Then you know I do not joke when I say this: let me pass or your death will be sudden and violent."

"F-forgive me . . . how could I know?"

"You know now," Raquella said icily. "You would do well to remember my voice."

Pushing past the girl, she led them off the jetty.

"Not bad," Carnegie whispered approvingly.

"I had a very good teacher."

Slattern Gardens was in fact a single, wide promenade flanked by the water's edge and a row of scrupulously tended townhouses. Elegantly orbed streetlamps warded off the permanent night of underground. Above the street, signs hanging from the townhouses jostled for position in the air, each one boasting of the priceless stones within. Jonathan looked in through a couple of windows, but all the shops appeared to be empty. The real business was taking place on the street outside.

The promenade was packed with women sashaying

down the Gardens in their finest dresses and gowns, their clothes and skin drenched in waterfalls of gems and diamonds. The light from the streetlamps reflected and refracted off the jewels, setting off a firework display of gold and silver that lit up the Gardens. At every turn women were talking excitedly to one another, but there was a sly undercurrent to the celebratory atmosphere. Some greeted old acquaintances with forced jollity, before turning away and whispering in the ears of their friends; some rebuffed friendly approaches with cool stares; others floated along in haughty solitude.

"OK. Where now?" said Raquella, under her breath, as they slipped through the stream of women.

"If memory serves, there's a shop called The Hearthstone three doors down. They know me. We should be safe there."

"STOP!"

The chatter and bustle of the Gardens ceased as an entire street froze. At the sound of the imperious voice, Carnegie muttered a particularly foul oath.

Peering out from underneath his cowl, Jonathan saw that the crowd had parted to reveal the woman who had hailed them. She was over six feet tall, with dark brown skin and dramatically cropped black hair. Unlike the other women who wandered down the Slattern Gardens, she was dressed simply in a silver waistcoat and trousers, a single matching diamond glowing in her left ear. Even so, as she strode forward, Jonathan was mesmerized. The woman was stunningly beautiful.

She wasn't alone. There were around twenty armed women with her, all dressed in the same flowing red robes that the girl on the jetty had worn. At the click of her fingers, they formed a threatening circle around the three intruders.

"You are Vendetta's maid," the woman said mildly. A statement, not a question. "I recognize you."

"I am honoured, Queenpin. My master has entrusted me to trade some stones on his behalf."

"Of course. All Darkside knows of your fidelity to Vendetta. But who are your companions?"

"New serving girls," Raquella said quickly. "He thought it best that I show them the Gardens."

The Queenpin ran a disdainful eye over Jonathan, who shrank back inside his hood. "By the looks of things, your master's judgement is not what it was."

Her eyes narrowed. When she spoke again, her voice was like a whip cracking across Jonathan's face.

"Remove your hood. Now."

8

Jonathan froze. The circle of guards tightened around them, a dazzling and deadly array of jewels and daggers, rings and swords. Even with Carnegie at his side, they wouldn't be able to fight their way out. If he took down his hood, they were as good as dead.

"I gave you an order," the Queenpin said, as icily beautiful as the diamond in her ear. "I don't expect to be kept waiting."

"Please forgive my cousin," Raquella cut in hastily, desperation creeping into her voice. "She is a deaf mute. She will not understand you."

The Queenpin gave her a scornful look. "How very trying. Why don't you be a good girl and remove the hood for her?"

"*Enough.*"

Carnegie stepped out into the centre of the ring. The wereman threw back his hood, exposing his craggy features to the gaslight. Gasps of shock and horror rose up from the

71

watching throng at the sight of a man, Slattern Gardens' greatest taboo.

"Let's end this charade," he snarled. "You know exactly who we are."

The Queenpin held his gaze steadily. "I know you're no woman. Did you really think you could creep around without being detected, wolfman? You know that no male may enter the Gardens while I rule. Was a cloak really enough? You can spend the remaining seconds of your life thinking about that. Guards, take them to my quarters."

Jonathan felt a knifepoint dig into his back, and several pairs of hands grabbed him. His hood was pulled off, to an encore of amazement from the crowd. He waited for a roar, the sounds of Carnegie hurling himself on to the attack, but to Jonathan's surprise the wereman mutely allowed himself to be manhandled by the guards. Between them, Raquella's face was grey. It seemed that she was to share the punishment of her male companions.

The procession carried along the glittering length of Slattern Gardens in a strained silence. As they were pushed and harried along the street, the crowds parted fearfully, as if the intruders carried some sort of infectious disease. Jonathan was too angry with himself to be afraid. He had failed, almost before he had started. What would happen to Mrs Elwood now? How would Alain cope, if he lost his son as well as his wife? And what about Theresa – was she still out there somewhere in Darkside, waiting in vain for Jonathan to find her? Would she even know that he had tried?

At the end of the promenade, the row of jewellery shops ran into a sheer rock face. A small boat was beached on the side of the street, looking out over the waterfront. It was a battered, bedraggled craft, coated in barnacles and peeling paint. The name *Silverine* was painted on its prow. The Queenpin climbed lithely up a ladder hanging down from the side and disappeared inside the cabin.

"She lives *here*?" Jonathan said in surprise. He was rewarded with a knife jab from one of the guards.

"Ow!"

"Speak with respect when you talk of the Queenpin," a young female voice hissed in his ear. "She has no need for luxury and fripperies. Now get up there."

She shoved Jonathan in the direction of the boat. Reluctantly, he hauled himself up the ladder, feeling the scratch on his back. The guards, he noted, waited below. It didn't make any difference – there was nowhere to run anyway. He ducked his head and entered the cabin, Raquella and Carnegie on his heels.

The interior of the *Silverine* was as cramped and shabby as its exterior. The floor listed sharply to one side, and bowed wooden planks groaned at the tread of Jonathan's feet. Charts and weapons covered the walls. The Queenpin was standing with her arms folded by a table next to the window, staring out over the water. When Carnegie entered the cabin, she immediately strode up to him and kneed him sharply in the groin.

As the wereman groaned and dropped to his knees,

Jonathan winced in sympathy. Expecting the wereman to lash out, he was amazed when instead Carnegie broke out into a weak chuckle.

"I was worried you hadn't missed me, Martha," he wheezed.

"Be silent," the Queenpin said coldly. "Your life hangs by a thread."

She paced up and down the cabin, glaring at Carnegie.

"Let me make sure I understand this. You trespass in my territory, breaking all the Gardens' rules, flaunting your presence with those *ridiculous* disguises. . ."

"Not for the first time," Carnegie interrupted mildly.

The Queenpin snorted. "That was a long time ago. You haven't graced us with your presence for several years."

Carnegie spread his hands out. "I've been busy, Martha. Look, I know the rules of Slattern Gardens better than anyone. I wouldn't have come here without a very good reason."

"And what would that be? More gambling debts? Are you penniless again?"

"If only it were that simple. I'm trying to help the boy here. He's had a run-in with Vendetta. He needs to get his hands on a certain jewel before the end of the week or someone's going to get hurt. We needed information, so we came here."

The Queenpin raised an eyebrow. "Since when have you cared about anyone other than yourself?"

Carnegie winced. "I'm not entirely selfish, you know," he said, sounding a little wounded. "And the boy and I are linked now – whether I like it or not. We have to get this jewel."

"And which particular stone would we be talking about?"

"The Crimson Stone!" Jonathan blurted out.

For a second the Queenpin looked startled. Then she burst out laughing.

"What is it?" Jonathan asked. "Have you heard of it?"

"Child, I run Slattern Gardens. The Crimson Stone is the most sought-after jewel in Darkside. Of course I have heard of it. I've spent years trying to track it down. And that sly old dog Gresham had it all the time! I sent a representative to the auction, but there was no way I could compete with Xavier's wealth. I thought that would be the last chance I had to see it. Of course, now I know differently," she said merrily, "because Vendetta's blackmailed a child into stealing it back from Xavier. Really, Elias. Even by your flimsy standards, this is a weak story."

"It's true!" Jonathan cried. "And I've only got six days left to get it or he's going to kill Mrs Elwood! You have to help us!"

"I don't have to do anything, child," said the Queenpin, in a tone eerily reminiscent of Carnegie. "And from now on you will stay silent unless I tell you." She turned to Raquella. "You work for Vendetta. Is this nonsense true?"

The maidservant nodded. "Yes, Queenpin. Jonathan has crossed my master in the past. I fear this is his revenge."

The ruler of Slattern Gardens thoughtfully tapped her cheek with a finger. Carnegie coughed pointedly.

"Yes?"

"There is one more thing," the wereman added. "Vendetta isn't working alone. He has joined forces with . . . Marianne."

The Queenpin's eyes blazed with hatred. She crashed a fist down on to the table, making all three of them jump.

"Now it starts to make sense. This sounds *exactly* like the kind of affair that scheming wench would involve herself in." She gave Jonathan an appraising stare. "You've made some powerful enemies."

"You don't know the half of it," he replied ruefully, and then, sensing an opportunity, "I'm sorry we trespassed here, Queenpin. But my friend's life is in danger. If you kill us, she'll die too."

The Queenpin turned back to the window, and the black, still waters outside.

"I could be persuaded to spare you," she mused.

"We need more than our lives, Martha," Carnegie growled. "We need your help."

She glanced back over her shoulder.

"My help comes at a price, Elias. What would you be willing to pay? How desperate are you? Would you beg for it?"

The wereman gave her a sardonic look.

"Hardly. But I would owe you."

"Would you now? What an interesting proposition." The Queenpin gestured at the table. "Sit. You will eat with me. We will discuss it then. In the meantime, Elias," she said, her eyes sparkling, "I'll have to think of some way you can repay me."

It was by some distance the strangest meal Jonathan had ever eaten: crowded round a rickety table in the cabin of a beached boat, illuminated by the prisms of lights shining forth from the promenade. Two young guards brought up platters of cold meat and vegetables and laid out a meal. Jonathan couldn't work out what he was eating, either by sight or taste, but made sure to look as if he was enjoying it. There was no cutlery, and everyone tucked in with their fingers. The Queenpin ate voraciously, tearing the meat into strips and stuffing it into her mouth, her chewing drowned out only by the sound of Carnegie's incisors tearing through flesh. When she disappeared to get more wine, Jonathan seized the chance to whisper a question to the wereman.

"Carnegie?" he said hesitantly. "Does she . . . *like* you?"

The wereman eyed him suspiciously. "Martha and I go back a long way."

"What, you used to go out?" Jonathan said incredulously.

"Put it this way," the wereman said mysteriously, wiping flecks of fatty meat from his chin, "before she met me, she used to wear two earrings."

Before Jonathan could ask anything further, the Queenpin returned to the table, swigging from a pitcher of wine.

"Let's talk business. You want to know which thieves you can approach. Now, as you can appreciate, no thief is reliable or trustworthy, but some are more skilled than others. I heard that Gracie Cartwright is between jobs – she knows her way around a safe. The Weston Boys are good too."

"We need more than good, Martha," Carnegie said. "We need the best."

"Well, you can't have the best," the Queenpin replied, matter-of-factly licking her fingers clean. "The Troupe split up five years ago."

"The Troupe?" asked Jonathan.

"Finest thieves I ever saw. They could get in and out of anywhere. To this day I still can't work out how they got hold of the Baskerville Emerald."

The wereman raised an eyebrow. "That was them?"

"I should know," the Queenpin smiled. "I bought it from them."

"Where are they now? Could we not try and get them back together?" asked Jonathan.

"You could try. It wouldn't be easy. But then, if anyone could get you the Crimson Stone, it would be the Troupe."

Carnegie stood up.

"Time to organize a reunion, then. Who do we start with?"

"With their leader. Antonio Correlli."

Jonathan's heart sank.

"Well, that's torn it," he said.

9

They slipped out of Slattern Gardens several hours later, after the shops had locked their doors, the gaslights had dimmed, and the ladies had returned to their Darkside dwellings. The broad expanse of the promenade was empty now, save for the four people heading back up towards the pier, led by a long-striding woman with a regal bearing.

In the perpetual darkness of the cavern, it was impossible to be certain what time it was, but Jonathan guessed it had to be early in the morning. His mind was a whirl of confusion. On the one hand, they had managed to escape the Gardens with their lives. On the other, it seemed that their best hope of recovering the Stone lay with Correlli – the fire-breathing mercenary Jonathan had clashed with only months beforehand. The last time they had met, a building burnt down around their ears, and he couldn't be sure that the mercenary was alive. Even if Correlli had survived, how could they persuade him to team up with them?

The waves were lapping against the base of the pier as

gently as a lullaby. Carnegie's gondola was now the only craft left in the water. The guard keeping watch at the edge of the jetty raised her dagger aloft in salute at the sight of her approaching leader. The Queenpin acknowledged her with a brisk nod.

"This is where we part company. I trust that you have learnt something about the Gardens tonight – and to respect its rules in future."

"Yes, Queenpin. Thank you," Jonathan said gratefully. "If we manage to get the Stone, it will owe a lot to you."

"If you manage to get the Stone, child," she replied, her eyes twinkling, "you will come and show me before you do anything with it, yes?"

Carnegie hustled Jonathan towards the gondola.

"Time permitting," he barked. "Come on, boy. Let's go and see if our old friend Correlli is still alive."

"Oh, he's alive all right," the Queenpin called out. "All Darkside's been talking about how a Lightside boy got the better of him. You might want to try the Sepia Rooms – I hear he's been spending a lot of time there recently."

As Jonathan and Raquella clambered down into the gondola, the wereman paused at the edge of the jetty. He turned back and clasped the Queenpin's elbow.

"If we get through this, Martha, you and I will meet up to discuss my debt. It has been fairly earned."

The Queenpin's eyes were bright. "Look after yourself, and the children. I shall take no pleasure hearing of your death, Elias."

Carnegie grinned, displaying his sharpened, feral teeth. "I think we both know that's not entirely true. Goodbye, Martha."

He sprang down on to the gondola and began to propel the boat onward, away from the jetty and deeper into Darkside. The Queenpin remained on the jetty for a few seconds, an indecipherable look on her face, before spinning on her heel and striding out of sight. Jonathan gave Carnegie a quizzical look and opened his mouth, but the wereman silenced him with a warning glare.

"Not a word, boy. Not a single word."

It was a drowsy, subdued journey back to the centre of Darkside. The gondola splashed out of the huge cavern, and down another long, narrow channel. Jonathan closed his eyes and rested his head against the side of the boat, lulled by the swelling of the waves. Beside him in the gondola, he heard Raquella humming a strange melody to herself. A strange calm washed over Jonathan, and he drifted quietly off to sleep.

He was jolted awake by a loud scream from somewhere high above his head. They had emerged from the dark channel into the open air, and were cutting through slightly deeper, choppier waters between two large wooden piers. The water was littered with all manner of flotsam and jetsam: rotten planks and rusted sheets of metal; dead fish; a small, flesh-coloured object that looked suspiciously like a human finger. Through the early morning mist, Jonathan could see dirty smudges of light in the sky.

A strong odour of salt and human waste hung in the air.

Jonathan sat up and rubbed his eyes. "Where are we?"

Carnegie took a deep breath.

"Judging by the smell, I'd say we were home. Devil's Wharf, to be precise."

A small makeshift platform had been constructed at the base of one of the piers, where a boy sat huddled in a blanket. Now struggling with the stronger current, Carnegie manoeuvred the gondola over towards the platform, and hurled the mooring rope to the boy. The young lad – who bore more than a passing resemblance to Philip, from beneath The Redblood – hailed the boat cheerily.

"Good morning, Mr Carnegie!"

The wereman gave him a suspicious glance as he stepped gingerly back on to dry land. "Hello, Peter. You were expecting us?"

"Yes, sir. Philip sent word that you were heading to the Gardens. Said that you'd probably end up here, if you made it out alive. And here you are! Good trip?"

"It had its moments," the wereman growled. "It would have been slightly easier with oars. When you see your brother, Peter, tell him I'd like a word. A very loud one, very close to his ear."

Peter nodded enthusiastically. "Will do, Mr Carnegie, sir. On my honour."

Carnegie shook his head wearily, clumped past the boy and began scaling the ladder that led up to the top of the pier.

*

Several hours later, they were standing on a street corner in a particularly rundown area of east Darkside. Jonathan had wanted to go straight from the pier to the Sepia Rooms, but Carnegie had insisted they return to his lodgings first. He claimed it was so they could rest, although Jonathan had a sneaking suspicion it was more to do with reclaiming his towering stovepipe hat.

The Sepia Rooms were located within a small, unassuming terraced house at the end of the street. No sign marked their presence – there wasn't even a number on the door. Heavy shutters guarded the windows. As Jonathan watched, a well-dressed man marched briskly up to the entrance, glanced quickly left and right, and then dived through the front door.

"Well, I guess that means they're open."

Carnegie gave him a grim look.

"The Sepia Rooms never close. The people in there don't really care what time it is." He straightened his hat. "Wait here. I'll be as quick as I can."

"Wait! You're not going in there without us!"

"Watch me. Look, boy, I've taken you to some fairly unpleasant places in Darkside, but I'm not going to be responsible for you going in there. You can wait for me outside. That's dangerous enough as it is."

To Jonathan's surprise, it was Raquella who answered.

"No," she said softly. "We're going with you. Don't you see, Carnegie? My life, and Jonathan's friend's life, depend upon finding this stone. You're the only one who *can* walk away. Wherever you go, we have to go too."

Carnegie rubbed his cheek uneasily. "I'm not happy about this."

"Neither am I," Raquella said gravely. "But this is how it has to be. Are you ready?"

The maidservant wrapped her shawl tightly around her shoulders and crossed the street. At the front door of the Sepia Rooms she paused for a second, head bowed, before turning the handle and entering the building. Carnegie and Jonathan hastened after her, and found themselves at the bottom of a flight of stairs. The door closed behind them with a resounding thump, like the lid of a sarcophagus. Raquella started to walk up the steps.

"Wait," the wereman said suddenly. "The air upstairs is going to make you feel strange. Cover your mouth with your sleeve, and try not to breathe too deeply. We leave when I say, and we don't stay a minute longer than we have to, OK?"

Jonathan and Raquella nodded seriously, and covered their mouths. The wereman sighed.

"Come on, then. Let's get this over and done with. I'll go first this time, though, miss."

The room upstairs was a hymn to lethargy. In the dim candlelight, men lay motionless on threadbare sofas, their eyes closed, their arms hanging limply down to the ground. There were well-to-do young men in dinner jackets, middle-aged tradesmen, vagrants in rags, united in the utter stillness. Ornate oriental screens depicted red and green dragons writhing and snapping at one another, and chasing their own tails. The air was thick with a sickly sweet odour. Even through the sleeve of his jacket, the pungent aroma made Jonathan's head swim.

He slowly skirted around the slumped form of a masked member of The Cain Club and moved deeper in the room, suddenly conscious of the effort it was taking to put one foot in front of the other. Already he was feeling light-headed, and the certainty of the floor and walls in the room seemed to be ebbing away. He peered cautiously at the faces around him, noting the same dreamy expression on every one. Carnegie and Raquella fanned out to widen the search, treading gingerly through the silent human wheatfield.

On a sofa in the corner of the room lay a thickset man in a deep reverie, his face obscured by a fleshy arm. Although the man shared Correlli's physique, Jonathan couldn't be sure it was the fire-eater. He picked his way over to the sofa and lifted the man's bulky arm as gently as possible. Instantly, he recognized the wiry hair and swarthy features. In the few months since he had last since him, Correlli had gone visibly downhill. His skin was pock-marked and etched with deep lines, and his breath smelt of stale alcohol.

Jonathan was just about to call over to Carnegie when the fire-eater's eyes snapped open and he lunged at Jonathan, arms outstretched.

10

Jonathan cried out and fell backwards on to the floor, landing awkwardly on a prone body. Correlli was on him in a flash, a pair of shovel-like hands fastening around his throat. As Jonathan struggled for breath, he heard Raquella scream from the other side of the room, and then a bestial roar. Black spots clustered in the corner of his vision, and he felt the strength begin to fade from his limbs. Then there was another roar, closer this time, and a blur of fur and claws crashed into Correlli, sending the pair of them flying across the room.

Jonathan rolled to one side in a coughing fit, his lungs desperately hunting for air. Too late, he remembered Carnegie's warning not to breathe too deeply inside the Sepia Rooms. Giant splashes of colour exploded in front of his eyes, and the room began to twist and spin around him until he felt like he was lying on the ceiling. He didn't know whether to cry or burst out laughing.

Something was shaking his arm.

"Jonathan, COME ON!" a female voice shouted. "Look!"

He staggered to his feet, trying to take in his surroundings. To his left, there was the snarling tangle of limbs that was Carnegie and Correlli. They were rolling across the floor, ignoring the slurred moans of the patrons as their drugged dreams were disturbed. Though the fire-eater was a formidable fighter, the atmosphere had dulled his reflexes, and he was facing a savage beast that thrived on combat. Already there was a deep cut running along Correlli's right arm.

"No!" Raquella cried, tugging at Jonathan's sleeve. "Over there!"

He looked round, blinking in surprise. A door had appeared in one of the screens, and a large Chinese man was bearing down upon them, his sleeves rolled up with threatening intent. A tattoo of a black dragon ran up his neck and over the top of his shaven scalp. He came to a halt in front of them, and loudly cracked his knuckles.

"These are my rooms. You are not welcome here," he said in a low voice. "You will leave now."

Before Jonathan could reply, he felt himself being hoisted up into the air by his shirt. The world didn't move with him, and his stomach lurched violently.

"Put him down!" Raquella screamed.

She aimed a sharp kick at his assailant's kneecap, but the man barely flinched. He casually tossed Jonathan to one side, sending him sprawling over one of the sofas, before turning his attention back to the maidservant.

"That was a very bad idea," the Chinese man said. "It nearly hurt."

Jonathan desperately wanted to close his eyes and go to sleep, until the pain and the dizziness and the nausea receded, but a voice in his head shouted at him to get up. He staggered to his feet and hurled himself at the man's back, but it was like running headlong into a brick wall. Jonathan simply bounced off him, the air whooshing from his lungs for the second time in a minute. As he tried to clear the cobwebs from his head, he looked up to see the man looming over him, his fingers curled up in a fist.

Jonathan closed his eyes, and waited for the darkness to fall. Instead, there was a loud crashing noise, and the thud of a large weight hitting the floor. He opened one eye cautiously. Raquella was standing over the body of the Chinese man, the remains of a shattered vase in one hand. Catching the look of shock on Jonathan's face, she shrugged.

"You looked like you could use some help. It was all that came to hand."

"Cheers," Jonathan said, rubbing his face groggily. "I had it under control, though."

A roar made them both whirl round. The beast had won its battle with Correlli, and the mercenary was lying unconscious on the floor, a nasty bruise on his temple. The beast raised a claw into the air, and prepared to strike.

"Carnegie, no!" cried Jonathan.

The beast stopped. A pair of blank, pitiless eyes sized the boy up.

"We need him, remember? If you kill him, we'll never get the Stone back!"

He was aware that, inside the beast's head, the remaining spark of Elias Carnegie's consciousness knew he was right. But the two opposing forces in the wereman's soul were constantly shifting and wrestling for control, and it was never certain which would hold sway. The beast flung Correlli to one side and swatted at the air, as if it was under attack from a swarm of bees. To Jonathan's horror, it then began to attack itself, gouging at its face, tearing its fur, jaws snapping at thin air. Raquella made as if to go towards him, but Jonathan put an arm across her path.

"We've got to do something!" she pleaded. "He'll kill himself."

"There's nothing we can do," he replied darkly.

Finally, the beast gave an almighty shudder, and its arms fell to its side. The powerful shoulders drooped, the fur retreated, and it was Carnegie crouching on the floor, panting heavily, his face bleeding from self-inflicted wounds.

"That," he rumbled, "was close."

"Are you OK?"

"Just dandy, boy. Now grab him and let's get out of this hellhole."

They dragged Correlli by his feet out of the Sepia Rooms, down the stairs and into the bright sunshine outside. The fresh air hit Jonathan like a sledgehammer. Letting go of the fire-eater, he leant over the wall and was violently sick. As he wiped his mouth on his sleeve, he became aware of Carnegie standing over him.

"I did tell you to wait outside," the wereman said, a trace of amusement in his voice. He prodded the prone form of Correlli with his toe. "At least we got what we came for."

"Great," Jonathan said bitterly. "He's not much use like this, is he?"

Carnegie frowned.

"Better wake him up then, hadn't we?"

Correlli woke up precisely two seconds after Carnegie hurled him from the pier at Devil's Wharf. Having hauled the prone fire-eater all the way from the Sepia Rooms, the wereman was in no mood to be gentle. Correlli's shocked yell was followed by a tremendous splash as the burly mercenary hit the waters below. Jonathan watched him sink beneath the surface with concern.

"You don't think he's going to drown, do you?"

"It's a possibility," Carnegie replied. "But Correlli's a survivor. He should be able to cope with an afternoon dip."

"Unless he can't swim," Raquella said.

The wereman chewed his lip thoughtfully. "I hadn't thought of that," he admitted.

Jonathan peered over the edge of the wharf, searching for a glimpse of Correlli beneath the murky waters. He was still suffering from the after-effects of the Sepia Rooms, and the churning and foaming of the waves stirred his stomach again. Worryingly, there was no sign of the mercenary.

Raquella glared at Carnegie, who cleared his throat with embarrassment.

"Don't look at me like that. I'm not going in after him."

There was another loud splash as Correlli exploded above the surface, frantically paddling to keep himself afloat as he took in a lungful of air.

"Told you he'd be fine," the wereman said defiantly.

He removed a lifebelt from its casing on the side of the wharf and cast it down on a rope towards Correlli. The fire-eater's survival instincts kicking in, he front-crawled through the choppy waves and slipped through the belt. Up on the wharf, Carnegie tied the rope around his waist and adopted a braced stance.

"Stand back," he said, through gritted teeth.

Then, hand-over-hand, he began hauling the mercenary out of the water and up through the air. When Correlli reached the edge of the wharf, Jonathan and Raquella helped to drag his sopping, flailing form on to the decking, where he lay panting, hair plastered to his forehead. Eventually he looked up and flashed the wereman a murderous glance.

"I'm . . . going to . . . kill you for this," he said haltingly.

"I need to talk to you," Carnegie replied, his coat flapping in the breeze. "I wanted to make sure I had your full attention."

"What on Darkside could you *possibly* want to talk to me about?

"We need to get our hands on something. We heard you were the man to talk to."

Correlli laughed bitterly. "What would I know? Ever since the boy defeated me I've been a laughing stock. Even pickpockets don't respect me any more. After so many years, so many crimes – a laughing stock."

Raquella kneeled down next to the mercenary. "We're offering you the chance to change that. If you can help us, no one will ever laugh at you again."

Correlli's eyes narrowed. "What exactly do you have in mind?"

"The crime of the century," she whispered, with a mischievous grin. "A crime that will be talked about for years to come. A crime that will make the Baskerville Emerald look like child's play."

"That's quite a claim," the mercenary said wistfully. "The Baskerville Emerald was the perfect robbery."

"We know you planned it," said Jonathan. "That's why we're here. We want you to come out of retirement and reform the Troupe."

Correlli waved him away with a hand. "The Troupe is history. If that's why you came to see me, you've wasted your time. I'll never work with them again."

"But you don't understand," Jonathan said desperately. "You have to help. My friend's life is at stake!"

"Really," he snapped. "And why should I care one

penny for your friend? I only wish it was your life at stake."

"Shall I throw him back in the water?" asked Carnegie.

He reached out to grab Correlli, who hastily held up both his hands.

"Wait a moment. This crime of the century. What's the target?"

Raquella cupped her hand and whispered into his ear. Correlli's look of astonishment was slowly succeeded by a broad grin.

"Really?" he said, with a chuckle. "Why didn't you say so?"

11

From a vantage point high up on a roof, London's skyline had a geography all of its own. In the surrounding Victorian terraced streets, the landscape of sharply inclined roofs was punctuated by television aerials and squat chimney stacks. Further afield, tower blocks and sky-scrapers competed for dominance of the air. In the distance, a heat haze had settled like sweat over the domed forehead of St Paul's Cathedral, and shimmered over the glass façade of the building Londoners called the Gherkin.

Jonathan Starling shielded his eyes from the glare and looked out anxiously over the skyline. "Are you sure they'll come?" he asked.

Correlli chewed on a piece of gum. "Yeah, they'll come. Whether they'll say yes or not is another matter."

Since agreeing to help them out, the fire-eater had regained some of his old menacing purpose. Immediately he had sent messengers out to his old Troupe members, arranging to meet them later that day. It had also been his idea to split up.

"It's the best way," he had argued as they hurried back from Devil's Wharf. "If Xavier's mansion is as heavily guarded as you say it is, we're going to need all the time we can get to check the place out. It makes sense if Jonathan and I head to Lightside, while you and the girl sort things out here. We can save nearly a day if we split up."

"Not so sure that's a good idea," Carnegie said warily.

Correlli stopped in his tracks, ignoring the jostling of the people around him.

"You asked for my help," he said finally. "I've said I'm in. But if you want to do this, you're going to have to trust me. OK?"

But, although they had reluctantly agreed to his plan, Jonathan couldn't pretend that he did trust the fire-eater. It was difficult to feel comfortable around someone who had recently tried to kill him. Over time he had become used to Carnegie's moods – he knew when to take a step back, or retire to another room. But Correlli kept himself to himself. It was impossible to tell what he was thinking. A suspicious voice in the back of Jonathan's mind wondered whether all of this was just a complicated ruse to get him alone and pay him back.

Given all of that, it wasn't surprising that they travelled back to Lightside in silence. Jonathan was becoming increasingly used to the sensation of crossing and, although his pulse quickened and his head throbbed, the feeling of sickness he had experienced in the past was absent. He was surprised to see that Correlli also seemed largely unaffected by the journey. Noting his quizzical look, the fire-eater shrugged.

"There's more than one half-Darksider in London, Jonathan."

And that, he hadn't been expecting at all. Biting back a barrage of questions, Jonathan allowed himself to be led through the streets to a terraced house in East London that the Troupe had used as a safe house in the past. It was dark and cool inside, with a stale odour that suggested it had lain empty for years. In the kitchen, Jonathan picked up a coffee mug filled with sprouting mould from the sideboard.

"Very homely."

The fire-eater gave him a warning glance. "We're meeting the twins up on the roof. Come on."

On the first-floor landing there was a skylight built into the ceiling. Correlli jumped up and slammed it open with a loud crash, before athletically flipping himself up through the gap and out on to the roof.

"There's a ladder in one of the bedrooms," he called down. "You might want to use that."

"Er, yeah. Cheers."

In a rather more laboured fashion, Jonathan clambered back into the sunshine, relieved to have escaped the musty gloom of the interior. The fire-eater had his back to him, and was scanning the horizon. Jonathan sat down on the edge of the roof, flicking tiny stones on to the street below.

"So how did you meet these guys?" he asked.

Correlli didn't turn round. "None of your business."

"Sorry," Jonathan replied sulkily. "I just thought it might be useful to know who the Troupe actually are. Seeing as we're going to be working together and all."

The fire-eater sighed, came over and sat down beside Jonathan. When he spoke, it was in a deep baritone.

"It started," he began, "with a bank job that went wrong. The heat was on, and I had to lie low for a while. I got off the Grand and went to Spinoza's Fairground on the edge of town – there's always work for fire-eaters at fairgrounds. My first day there, I watched the trapeze act: the twins, Fray and Nettle. When I saw those girls fly through the air, the first thing I thought was that it was the most incredible thing I had ever seen. The second thing I thought was that they would make supreme burglars. And I was right, too – if there's a building they can't climb and find a way into, then I haven't seen it. Anyway, it suddenly hit me – I could put a crack team of thieves together right there in the circus, using the special skills of the different performers. The twins didn't take much persuading, and after that it was fairly simple."

"Who else did you ask?"

"Well, I figured if we were going to steal stuff, we needed a getaway driver, and there was only one man for that job. Verv was the fastest and craziest stunt rider at the fairground. No one could handle a horse like he could. Of course, the fact that he was crazy helped. The only thing that mattered to him was speed. A good job, too. We'd have been caught a couple of times if it hadn't been for him. And then . . ."

Correlli closed his eyes.

". . . and then there was Mountebank. Swine. A two-bit card shuffler calling himself a magician. Not that I knew that at Spinoza's. Back then, he looked like the final piece of the puzzle. He could pick a lock with his eyes closed. Doors, safes . . . nothing could keep him out. I wouldn't learn about the other side to him until much later. . ."

His voice trailed off, and he hurled a stone far off the edge of the roof.

"We went to work right away. And we were *good*. I selected the target, the twins got us in, Mountebank got us the goods, and Verv got us out again. Some of our jobs went so smoothly it was like the victims were helping us. The Baskerville Emerald was the best example of that. It was secured in a safe, surrounded by a ring of bodyguards in a locked strongroom. How did we steal it without anyone seeing us? Even I'm not sure, and I planned it.

"In the end, that turned out to be our final job. Verv and the twins crossed over to Lightside while Mountebank went back to performing in Darkside, and I . . . well, you know what I ended up doing."

"But why?" said Jonathan, suddenly curious. "You'd just pulled off your greatest robbery. Why split up then?"

Correlli was spared the need to reply by a flash of movement on top of a house a couple of streets away.

The fire-eater got to his feet, brushing the back of his trousers.

"Here they come. Right on time."

Straining his eyes, Jonathan could just make out two figures racing over a rooftop. They were running at full speed across the peak of the roof, their feet blurring across the thin ledge. One swung around an aerial, while the other executed a neat backflip over a chimney stack. The two women were mirror images of one another, dressed in modern clothing – three-quarter-length tracksuit trousers and vest tops – with short, boyish blonde haircuts.

"Remember," Correlli added, "if you're having trouble telling them apart, Nettle's the prickly one."

"That shouldn't be too hard to remember."

The fire-eater gave him an amused look, but said nothing.

The twins had reached the adjacent building, which was separated from the safe house by a ten-foot gap. Jonathan was about to ask the fire-eater how they were going to get across it when, without breaking stride, both women leapt into the air. Jonathan gasped. They arced gracefully through the sky, soaring impossibly high before hurtling down towards the safe house. Landing in a cloud of dust several paces away from Jonathan and Correlli, both twins slipped smoothly into a forward roll to lessen the impact. The woman on the left was up on her feet instantly, jabbing her finger into her twin's side.

"Call that a jump? You nearly took me down with you, you fat pig!"

"You poke me again, you'll lose your finger!"

"What are you going to do – eat it?"

Correlli coughed. The twins whirled round. Two sly smiles appeared on their faces, their argument instantly forgotten. They moved lithely towards the fire-eater.

"Well, well . . ."

". . . well. Antonio Correlli. It's been a while."

"A long while," her sister concurred. "*Too* long a while, Fray?"

Fray frowned, considering the question.

"No," she said slowly, "I wouldn't say that, exactly."

Correlli bowed extravagantly. "Ladies. It is wonderful to see you both again. These past years have been poorer for the lack of your company."

Nettle gave him a scornful look. "Save that rubbish for your thru'penny wenches, Correlli. Or Fray."

Her sister yanked her hair sharply.

"OW!"

"You're the only wench around here, Nettle!"

They clenched their fists and stood off against one another. Correlli held his hands up for calm.

"Please . . . both of you. You can sort this out later. We have an interesting proposition for you, and there isn't much time."

"We?" they said, in chorus. For the first time, the twins noticed Jonathan's presence. A look of disdain spread over both their faces.

"Who's . . ."

". . . *that*?"

"I'm Jonathan," he replied calmly.

Fray put her hand over her mouth in a fake display of horror. "Watch out, Correlli. We've heard that children can be bad for your health."

"Especially *your* health," her sister chimed in.

The twins fell about laughing, the sound of high-pitched giggling echoing out over the rooftops.

"Hilarious," Correlli said drily, as their giggles subsided. "It's good to know that word of my humiliation has crossed over to Lightside. More importantly, did you hear about the Crimson Stone?"

The twins' faces went abruptly serious.

"Such a waste," Fray said sadly. "Such an amazing thing . . ."

". . . going to such a wrinkly old man," her twin concluded.

"Well, then maybe this might be of interest to you." Correlli drew himself up. "I'm going to help the boy pinch it, and I need your help to do it."

The two girls glanced at each other, communicating without saying a word. Then they took up a position on each side of the fire-eater, taking it in turns to whisper into his ear.

"You do know . . ."

". . . stealing's wrong, don't you?"

"What's in it . . ."

". . . for us?"

"The boy gets the Crimson Stone," replied Correlli calmly. "We get everything else. Xavier's a hoarder, and a wealthy one to boot. Whatever's in there is going to be worth a pretty penny."

Colour rushed to both of the twins' cheeks.

"Will there be diamonds . . ."

". . . and rubies? Rubies are my favourite."

"Going on Xavier's reputation, I'd imagine that every stone under the rainbow will be there. Is that enough to tempt you?"

The twins scampered over to the edge of the roof and formed an impromptu huddle. Their whispers grew louder and louder, until one of them – Jonathan had no idea which – shrieked with anger.

"Take that back!"

Correlli rolled his eyes.

"This may take some time," he said, out of the corner of his mouth.

12

It felt like the longest afternoon of Raquella's life. Perched in a chair in Carnegie's lodgings, she stared at a grandfather clock, willing the minute hand to move more quickly around the dial. Until the magician Mountebank began his evening performance at Kinski's Theatre of the Macabre, there was nothing for them to do. Even so, as she sat there, Raquella could almost hear the sands of time pouring away. With their deadline drawing closer, it seemed foolish to waste even a second. She wanted to get up and go outside into the cramped, noisy streets – to do something, *anything*. At least Jonathan had been able to go back to Lightside immediately. He wasn't just waiting.

By comparison, Carnegie was a picture of calm. He was sprawled out on the divan, flicking through a penny dreadful. The garish cover of the magazine was drenched in red ink, its title proclaiming *Gruesome Tales of Spring-Heeled Jack*. Occasionally a rumbling chuckle escaped from the wereman's throat. He looked up as – not for the first time that afternoon – Raquella tutted.

"No point getting worked up," he rumbled. "No doubt we'll be in mortal danger soon enough."

"It would almost be a relief! Anything's got to be better than all this waiting around. Carnegie, it's Saturday already. We've only got five days to get Vendetta the Stone."

"Which means we're in for a busy time. Until then, you should try and relax." Carnegie propped himself up on one arm, and waved the magazine around his lodgings. "Don't you see? Sitting around waiting is the good bit. The bit with the fighting and the nearly dying is the bad bit. Try not to confuse the two."

"I guess you're right." She nodded at the penny dreadful. "Good read?"

The wereman snorted. "It's utter rubbish. It beats staring at the clock, though. Want to read it after me?"

Raquella shook her head. "If it's all the same, I think I'd rather stay tense."

"Fair enough."

Carnegie settled back into his penny dreadful, reading until his eyelids dropped and he fell fast asleep. The magazine slipped from his fingers on to his chest, where it rose up and down on his undulating ribcage. From time to time, he growled softly in his sleep. At nine o'clock, as the light began to fade and the shadows began to thicken inside the room, Raquella gently shook him awake.

"It's time," she said.

The wereman's teeth glinted in the gloom. "Let's go and twist the magician's arm, then."

He rose like a ghost and headed for the front door. Outside, they hastened through the dingy enclave of Fitzwilliam Street and out on to the broad pavements of the Grand. It was still early on Darkside's cankerous main street, and it would be several hours until the first argument began, the first punch was thrown, and the first score was settled. Even so, the pavements were thronged with people sweating and steaming in the summer heat, and boisterous shouts ricocheted off the surrounding buildings. Outside The Last Supper, an ornate carriage came screeching to a halt and belched out a group of portly, well-dressed diners, who hastened inside the restaurant before they could be waylaid. In the gutter by the Casino Sanguino, an old man held up his last, blood-drenched coin, whimpering quietly to himself. From somewhere deep within the bowels of the Psychosis Club, the sound of a lone violin playing an off-key dirge drifted up on to the street.

Over the years, both Carnegie and Raquella had become well-known faces in Darkside, and as they walked along the Grand, more than one head turned. They made an odd couple – the rangy, down-at-heel private detective and the small, purposeful maidservant. Yet, in different ways, they both signalled trouble. Aware of the whispers that ran through the crowds like a sea breeze, Carnegie simmered and snarled at anyone foolish enough to pay too close an inspection.

Fearful that the wereman's temper was about to erupt, Raquella was relieved when Kinski's Theatre of the Macabre came into view. A tall, gravely elegant building, it occupied centre stage of the Grand. A row of stone steps led up to a grand entrance framed by flaming torches. Craning her neck, Raquella could see a row of balustrades running along the length of the first-floor balcony, before the top of the building was swallowed up by the night sky. On the pavement in front of the theatre, a large drunk man in a herald's costume was trying to drum up trade.

"Dare you come inside?" he bellowed. "Dare you enter the occult world of Mountebank the Magnificent – the Master of the Macabre, the man who has outwitted the Devil himself? His feats of magic will astound and amaze! The faint of heart should keep on walking!"

Despite the increasing volume and slurring of speech, no one in the crowds swelling past the theatre gave the herald a second glance.

At the entrance, a bored elderly woman was sitting in a ticket booth. Carnegie swept straight past her.

"Oi!" she squawked indignantly. "Where d'you think you're going, sonny?"

"Inside," he said ominously.

"It'll cost you a farthing a head."

Carnegie patted his waistcoat pockets, and gave Raquella a sideways glance. The maidservant sighed and handed over two coins.

"You're a real gentleman," she told the wereman.

"You'll get it back," he replied, affronted. "I always pay my debts."

"I'll believe that when I see it."

Compared to its grand façade, the foyer of Kinski's had seen better days. The tatty green carpet was covered in large stains, and there was a strong odour of cheap alcohol. The walls were covered with torn posters advertising such varied delights as *The Bloody Bard, Dr Faust's Chorus of Devils* and *Susie, Snake Charmer Extraordinaire*. Raquella wondered how it had looked when the theatre had first opened, whether the brass had gleamed and the lights had shone brightly, or whether the foyer had been as grubby as it was now.

Carnegie surveyed the scene with distaste. "Nice."

"Have you not been here before?" Raquella asked with surprise.

"I'm not what you'd call a theatre-goer. Come on – we've missed the start of the show."

He pushed through a set of double doors and into the auditorium. It was a vast space, row upon row of seats stretching away from the main stage. Boxes ran around the sides of the hall. The high ceiling was covered in a detailed, bloody frieze of clowns fighting with one another. The auditorium was all but empty, with only a handful of heads visible in the seats down near the stage. The echoes of past performances, the raucous applause, laughter and cheers of the audience had long since died away, replaced with a mournful atmosphere of loss.

Mountebank the Magnificent was standing alone on

stage. He was a striking sight. There was not a drop of colour in his skin, and his head was covered in a thin layer of white hair. His eyes were a piercing blood-red. He was dressed in a dazzling white suit that accentuated his pale skin tone, with a matching bright pink handkerchief poking out of his breast pocket.

As Raquella and Carnegie settled into seats towards the back of the auditorium, he clapped his hands, and suddenly a raven was flying around the auditorium, cawing loudly. It circled higher and higher into the air before returning to the stage and settling on the magician's shoulder. He bowed in the face of non-existent applause.

"You are too kind. Thank you. Now, for my most dazzling feat of magic, I will need a fearless assistant. Let me see. . ." He scanned the sparse crowd. "How about that young lady . . . there?"

Mountebank pointed straight at Raquella. She groaned and slunk lower into her seat.

"Oh great. What should I do now?" she hissed.

"Get up there," Carnegie murmured back. "He's the man we've come to see, isn't he? Perfect way to meet him."

Raquella rose reluctantly from her seat, a shove from the wereman sending her stumbling into the aisle. There was a half-hearted round of applause from the audience. Cursing her bad luck, she walked self-consciously towards the front of the auditorium, where Mountebank gave her a charming smile and helped her up on to the stage. His hand, she noted, was deathly cold to the touch.

"Thank you, my dear. What's your name?"

"Raquella," she said, feeling suddenly very small under the harsh glare of the footlights.

"Really? What an unusual name!" Mountebank replied lightly. "Well, Raquella, you shall have the honour of helping me with my finest trick. It's a card trick." There was a groan from the audience. He held up a hand. "Please. I'll think you'll find it's as unusual a card trick as this young lady's name."

Raquella blinked. Suddenly there was a pack of cards in the magician's hand. He fanned them out and then turned his head away.

"Please pick one and show the audience – make sure I can't see it! Then sign the card and put it back in the pack."

Eager to get off the stage, Raquella quickly selected a card and looked at it. The cold face of the Queen of Knives stared back at her. For some inexplicable reason, it sent a shiver of fear down her spine. She flashed the card to the audience and then signed it before slipping the Queen of Knives back into the fanned pack. Mountebank smiled, and the cards disappeared as quickly as they had arrived.

"Expertly done! Thank you, my dear."

Raquella curtsied and made to leave the stage, but the magician grabbed her hand.

"If you could help me with just one more thing. To complete this trick, I will need the help of my patented card-picking machine."

There came a rumble of wheels from the wings, and

then a giant contraption appeared on the stage, pushed by two assistants dressed in black hooded costumes. They looked horribly like executioners. With a great show of ceremony, Mountebank donned a white hood of his own, and led Raquella over to his "patented card-picking machine". Up close, she could see that it was a steel table, above which hung a canopy of gleaming metal spikes. There were leather straps at each corner of the table.

"R-really," Raquella stammered. "I'm not so sure about this. . ."

"Relax, my dear," he replied, taking her firmly by the wrist. "I've performed this trick thousands of times. It's only gone wrong once or twice."

Nobody laughed. A murmur of expectation rippled through the hall.

Mountebank made her lie down on the table and began fastening the straps around her legs and ankles, talking to the audience all the while.

"You see, to get the heart of your choice, my machine has to get to the heart of you. And it does so with these special 'mind readers' here."

The magician flicked one of the spikes, which gave off a metallic twang. Finishing with the final ankle strap, he leant over Raquella and whispered, so softly that only she could hear it:

"No one comes to my show late." His eyes flashed dangerously through the slits in his hood.

"What?"

With a flourish, the magician drew a curtain across the machine and headed back to the front of the stage. Raquella looked up with horror at the army of spikes looming over her.

"One of the first rules of magic, ladies and gentlemen, is that appearances can be deceptive. This is more than just a mere card trick. There is a life at stake here."

Raquella began to struggle, but the straps were tightly bound, and there was no room for manoeuvre. The magician's sonorous voice was growing in volume, filling the hall.

"Watch in horror as Mountebank the Macabre performs the most dangerous magic trick in Darkside. May the Ripper have mercy on her should it go wrong."

"No, please! Carnegie!"

"NOW!"

There was a click, and then the spikes came hurtling down. Raquella screamed.

13

Late night outside King's Cross station, and suddenly Jonathan was grateful for the presence of Correlli alongside him, the fire-eater's arms folded menacingly across his bare chest. Fray and Nettle had slipped back to their room to collect their things – still bickering and finger pointing, but seemingly on side. Now they were waiting for the other Troupe member, Verv. Looking around nervously, Jonathan wished he would hurry up. Though the Euston Road was just another wide, nondescript London thoroughfare, at this time of night there was an ugly edge to the atmosphere: angry drunken shouts, scuffles, figures skulking in doorways. Every few minutes, a police car dashed past them, its siren screaming. Jonathan pulled his hood up and tried to melt into the shadows.

After what seemed like an age, the street echoed to the sound of an engine roaring like a scalded dragon. As two powerful beams pierced the night, Correlli drew himself up expectantly.

"Here he comes."

The roaring grew louder, and the headlights brighter. Jonathan could make out the shape of a vehicle heading down the street towards them. Whatever it was, it was moving *fast*.

"Are you sure he's going to stop?" he asked doubtfully.

"One way or another," Correlli replied, and stepped out into the middle of the road.

"Is that a good idea?" Jonathan called out. "He's going pretty fast. . ."

By way of reply, the fire-eater adjusted his waistcoat and ran a hand through his wiry hair, calmly facing the onrushing vehicle like a matador at a bullfight. The car was now only a hundred yards away, and devouring the road. Expecting the driver to start applying the brakes at any second, Jonathan was horrified to see the car surge eagerly forward.

"He's speeding up!" he cried. "He's going to kill you!"

The car was fifty yards away. Correlli didn't flinch, didn't blink.

"Get out of the way!"

Twenty yards away. Jonathan shut his eyes, unable to watch. There was a squeal of brakes, but too late, far too late. He tensed, waiting to hear a sickening thud. When none came, he opened his eyes and blinked with surprise.

Somehow Correlli was still standing unharmed in the middle of the road. The car had come to rest some two inches from him, the front bumper nearly brushing his shins, lying at the fire-eater's feet like a dutiful dog. Almost as an afterthought, Jonathan realized that the car was a London cab – though not like any other cab he had seen before. It was painted a dark maroon colour, with tongues of flame licking the wheel arches and the bottom of the bodywork. The TAXI sign on the roof of the car was dark.

Correlli banged on the bonnet, smiling.

"You've got slack," he shouted out to the driver. "You used to get much closer to me than that."

The door opened, and out bounded a skinny young man wearing a leather jacket. His hair was sculpted into a towering bright pink Mohican that blazed in the headlights. When he spoke, it was in an excitable, high-pitched voice.

"You're getting on, bossman. Didn't want to make your ticker go ka-boom!"

He clutched at his chest in an exaggerated mime of a heart attack, and collapsed on to the road.

"Very thoughtful of you, Verv," Correlli said drily.

Verv remained kicking and convulsing for a few seconds, and then lay very still. He giggled and raised his head.

"Anyone want a lift?"

Behind the wheel, Verv was a figure of perpetual motion. As the cab careered through the streets of London, he bounced up and down in his seat, headbanging, drumming on the steering wheel and whooping with joy. Sitting beside him, Jonathan was transfixed by the speedometer, which never dropped below a hundred. Every traffic light they passed through was green, and no queues of cars held them up. It was as if the city had opened up for Verv. Even so, every time they hurtled around a sharp corner, Jonathan had to fight the urge to cling on to something.

"Hey! Hey!"

Verv swivelled in his seat and leant towards Jonathan, his hair like a Day-Glo shark's fin.

"You know best thing about Lightside?"

The cab was bearing down on a tramp staggering across the road. Jonathan pointed frantically.

"Watch out for that guy!"

Without taking his eyes from the boy, Verv spun the steering wheel through his hands and smoothly swerved round the tramp.

"Tarmac!" he bellowed, beating the roof of the cab. "I *love* tarmac."

He squeezed down on the accelerator pedal and the car leapt forward again.

"Cobbled streets are no fun. Here I can go super-fast – *quickety-quick.*"

"No kidding," Jonathan said meaningfully.

"Me fastest cabbie in the whole city," Verv proclaimed proudly. "Free ride, too."

"They must love you round here," Correlli called out from the back seat.

A sad look came over Verv's face.

"Lightsiders rude," he said. "They too busy screaming and being sick to thank me."

"So what's the deal, bossman?"

Verv opened his fourth sachet of ketchup and poured it over his chips, his right foot tapping out a furious drumbeat on the tiled floor. They were sitting in the neon glow of a fast-food restaurant, the cab cooling off in the car park outside. This late at night, the place was all but empty, save for a couple of bored attendants, an arguing couple, and a man slumped over on a table, snoring. Having jabbered his order to the man behind the counter, Verv was now struggling to fit four burgers, three cartons of chips and an extra-large milkshake on to his tray. Jonathan felt queasy just looking at his meal.

Correlli shifted awkwardly, wedged uncomfortably into an undersized plastic chair.

"One job. One night. Unimaginably high security. Unlikely that all of us will get out alive."

Verv's eyes widened. He took a giant bite out of a burger.

"Cool!" he said, spraying Jonathan with pieces of processed meat. "Be like old times. Be like Baskerville job." He thrust a handful of chips into his mouth and chewed reflectively. "Me drive so fast that night. . ."

Correlli's face darkened at the mention of the Baskerville robbery.

"So you're in?" he asked, brusquely.

Verv chuckled. "I'm in . . ."

Jonathan let out a small sigh of relief.

". . . on one condition."

"Which is?"

Verv took a deep slurp from his milkshake, his eyes bright with adrenalin.

"Bossman race me first."

Back behind the wheel of his cab, Verv dusted off his hands and swallowed his last mouthful. His mouth was ringed with ketchup, which in the dark looked horribly like blood. Instinctively Jonathan thought of Vendetta, and shuddered. Verv wound down the window.

"You ready?"

The fire-eater sighed. "I guess so. We're racing down Euston Road, one lap around Regent's Park and then the first one to pass through Marble Arch wins, right?"

"But this isn't fair!" Jonathan protested. "We're on foot and you're in that thing!"

"Yeah, but me go get the twins too. They live *long* way out of town. You got loads of time to get a lift. Plenty of cars in London. Just ask!"

"That's as maybe, Verv," Correlli replied wearily. "But this is still an unbelievable pain."

"Don't be mean, bossman. It's more fun this way!"

He flicked a switch, and suddenly the TAXI light on top of the cab lit up. The cab driver winked at Jonathan.

"Might take a fare on the way. Ciao!"

The cab screeched away in a wreath of smoke, filling the air with the smell of burning rubber. Correlli stood motionless as it flew out of the car park, nearly rising up on to two wheels.

"What are we waiting for?" Jonathan cried. "He's getting away!"

The fire-eater waved him away. "Be quiet. I'm thinking. We'll never beat Verv in a straight race. We need to out-think him."

He punched his fist into his palm. "Right. I know. Let's go."

And with that, Correlli began to run.

At first Jonathan was surprised by how quickly the burly fire-eater thundered along the backstreets, but he soon slipped into a natural running rhythm, and matched Correlli stride for stride. It was almost enjoyable, haring down the pavements in the centre of the city, through the shadows of deserted office blocks, their footsteps echoing in tandem. Then Jonathan thought of Verv charging towards the finishing line at a hundred miles an hour, and he wondered how they could hope to beat him.

As they headed west, the lights became brighter, and the streets busier. Jonathan realized that they were entering Soho, the heart of London nightlife, where the bars and restaurants stayed open well into the early morning. Correlli came to a halt by a giant oriental arch that looked down the length of a broad pedestrianized street filled with people. A group of rickshaws had been pulled over underneath the arch, and a gaggle of men were talking and laughing with one another. Panting slightly, the fire-eater approached them and called out:

"Rufus?"

A tall, muscular man stepped forward and nodded at Correlli. "Hello, Antonio. It's been a while. In a rush?"

"No time to explain. Marble Arch, as fast as you can."

Rufus nodded, and ushered them into his rickshaw. His bulging arms lifted up the carriage as if it were a toy, and then, with a silent heave, he began to pull them forward. Gradually the rickshaw picked up speed, until it was keeping pace with the cars on the road. Startled by the rate at which they were travelling, Jonathan looked down at Rufus's legs, which were galloping like a racehorse. Amidst the blurring, it looked for all the world as if there were more than two limbs moving.

Jonathan shot Correlli a questioning glance.

"Rufus is an old friend from back home," the fire-eater explained. "He's the fastest thing on three legs. Verv drives incredibly fast, but the twins live miles away. If we forget about Regent's Park and take a shortcut, we might be able to beat him to Marble Arch. And that's all that matters."

The rickshaw ride through Soho was a blur of faces, shouts from startled passers-by, garish window displays and neon lights. Rattling around in the back, Jonathan felt every bump and every pebble in the road. He couldn't help but marvel at the speed with which Rufus weaved in and out of the traffic. When they burst out of the winding alleys of Soho and on to the wider Oxford Street, the rickshaw managed to pick up even more pace. Deaf to the horns of angry bus drivers, Rufus raced west.

Eventually the road widened, and up ahead Jonathan saw an island in the middle of a busy intersection of roads. On the island, a squat white structure gazed solemnly down at the cars swarming around its base: Marble Arch. To Jonathan's amazement, Verv was nowhere to be seen. He nudged Correlli.

"I don't believe it! We're going to win!"

From behind him came a familiar throaty roar. Jonathan twisted in his seat to see the flame-painted cab speeding down Oxford Street after them, headlights on full beam.

"Spoke too soon! He's coming! Rufus!"

Rufus bowed his head and strained even harder, hauling the rickshaw forward again, but the cab loomed ever closer on their tail, sounding blasts on its horn as if it were on a hunt. Verv brushed his bumper against the back of the rickshaw, sending Rufus stumbling forward. Looking behind him and through the cab's windscreen, Jonathan could see the driver grinning manically and headbanging to some unheard beat. As they reached the traffic lights before the intersection, Verv pulled out from behind them and moved to the right, primed to overtake.

But not, as it turned out, in time.

In a final, daredevil manoeuvre, Rufus galloped through a red light and cut across the stream of cars heading in the other direction, before executing a wild left turn and hurtling up on to the island and underneath Marble Arch. Equally mindless of his own safety, Verv zoomed through the traffic and crashed through the arch millimetres after them, coming to a skidding halt on the broad promenade beyond.

Suddenly everything was very quiet. Correlli blew out his cheeks with relief, and patted the exhausted Rufus on his back. Jonathan peeled himself from his seat and climbed out of the rickshaw, relieved to feel the broad paving stones beneath his feet. Above his head, the national flags that lined the promenade were gently fluttering in the night breeze. Jonathan walked slowly over to the cab and got into the front seat, where he was surprised to see Verv humming cheerily to himself, tapping on the steering wheel. In the back seat, Fray and Nettle were sitting with their arms folded, pointedly looking out of opposite windows. When he saw Jonathan, Verv giggled and whispered in his ear.

"Bossman *is* getting old. Had to wait twenty minutes for you to show up."

Jonathan stared at him, dumbfounded.

"You threw the race? Why – what was the point. . .?"

Verv simply whooped, banged the roof of his cab, and revved up his engine once more.

14

Suddenly Raquella was tumbling down a narrow chute, her arms and legs banging against the sides. From somewhere above her head there was a deafening clang, and then she landed with a thump on something soft, sending a cloud of feathers into the air. The maidservant lay dazed for a second, and then sneezed violently.

Gingerly, Raquella got to her feet and surveyed her surroundings. She had fallen into a small room underneath the stage. An old mattress had been laid on the ground to break her fall. At the top of the chute, the underside of the steel table appeared as solid and immovable as it had been before, but the leather straps that had pinned her down were now dangling uselessly from her wrists and ankles, and the sound of enthusiastic applause was filtering down from the auditorium.

"Thank you! Thank you!" she heard Mountebank cry. "It is indeed the Queen Of Knives! My machine never fails! Till next we meet. . .!"

There was the sound of an explosion, and then a gasp of surprise from the audience.

"Stupid magician," Raquella muttered to herself, as she undid the straps from her wrists. "I'll make him disappear."

"Er . . . excuse me, miss?"

She looked up. A door had opened and a boy of Raquella's age was peering into the room. He had a cloth cap on his head, and his face was covered in what looked like soot.

"What?" she snapped.

"Are you OK? Soft landing?"

"Never better. Who are you?"

"Samuel Northwich. You can call me Sam."

He waited expectantly.

"Raquella Joubert," the maid said finally. "You can call me Miss Joubert."

"Oh, right. Well, I'm Mr Mountebank's apprentice. I'm here to take you to his dressing room. He always wants to say thank you to people who've helped him out with a trick."

"How generous of him. Lead the way. There's a few things I'd like to say to him myself."

Raquella smoothed down her hair and headed after the boy with as much dignity as she could muster. He scampered through a network of corridors that ran underneath the theatre, respectfully doffing his cap as they passed dressing-room doors tattooed with pentagrams and the word "Star" scrawled beneath them. Backstage, it was as if

123

all the theatre's productions were taking place at once: Raquella had to duck down as a team of jugglers hurled knives at one another out in the hallway, swerve out of the way as a clown pursued a fleeing rabbit, and step over the prone form of a suited gentlemen lying on a bed of nails, reading a copy of *The Darkside Informer*.

Eventually the corridor became quieter and dingier, and the cacophony of rehearsals faded away to nothing. They came to a halt by two doors facing each other at the end of the corridor. A puddle of brown water was seeping out from underneath one. The boy opened the other and grandly gestured for Raquella to enter.

"*This* is the dressing room of Mountebank the Magnificent?" asked the maidservant, her voice heavy with irony.

"'S'not so bad," the boy said loyally. "If he wants to use the loo, it's just across the hall."

"I'm sure that's a great comfort," she murmured.

Compared to the scene outside, Mountebank's dressing room was surprisingly warm and welcoming. It was bursting at the seams with props and gadgets: coloured scarves and magic lanterns; top hats and giant playing cards. A collection of swords leant idly against a large cabinet decorated with stars. Near to the door, a pristine mirror hung over a dressing table cluttered with make-up.

"He's got a lot of stuff in here, hasn't he?"

"This is a treasure trove, miss," Sam replied reverently. "There's enough tricks in here for ten magicians. But Mr

Mountebank only uses the best. That's what sets him apart from the others. They'll do any cheap stunt to get an audience. My master respects magic."

Given the size of Mountebank's audience, Raquella couldn't help wondering whether other magicians had the right idea, but she was touched by the passion in Sam's voice.

"If you wait here, miss, Mr Mountebank'll be along presently."

He paused, seemingly unwilling to leave her alone with all the props. Raquella looked at him thoughtfully.

"You do know your face is covered in soot, don't you?"

The boy peered in the mirror, his eyes widening with shock. "Oh no! He'll kill me if he finds out!"

"If he finds out what?"

Sam located a dog-eared handkerchief from the recesses of his pockets, spat on it, and vigorously rubbed his face.

"It's not soot, miss. It's explosive powder. I was trying to do one of Mr Mountebank's illusions, The Exploding Death, when . . . it went sort of wrong. He hates me messing around with stuff. Aw, it's not coming off!"

Raquella rolled her eyes. "Oh, for Darkside's sake, come here!"

She removed a clean handkerchief from her sleeve, doused it in a glass of water on the dressing table and began to wipe Samuel's face clean, ignoring the boy's winces and wriggles.

"Stop moving about. . .!"

"I can't help it – it tickles."

Though the powder was coming off, underneath it had left a residue that had stained Samuel's freckled skin a sour nicotine yellow.

"I can't get rid of this. It'll need carbolic soap and a scrubbing brush."

Samuel shuddered. "I'm going to have to go before he gets here." He ran out of the room, calling out over his shoulder, "Whatever you do, don't touch anything!"

Raquella scrunched up the dirty handkerchief and tossed it amongst the clutter. Boys were such odd creatures sometimes. She barely had time to find herself a seat before the door opened again, and Mountebank strode triumphantly in. There was a sheen of perspiration across the magician's forehead, and he was slightly out of breath, but he was smiling. Carnegie was following close behind. Unusually for the wereman, he was grinning too.

"You should have seen it, Raquella!" he said. "After you disappeared, Mountebank pulled up the spikes, and your card was stuck on one of them. Then there was an explosion and he disappeared! If I'd known the theatre was this much fun, I would have come before."

The magician gave him a benevolent smile. "I'm glad you enjoyed the performance. It did go rather well tonight."

He stopped, noticing the glare on the maidservant's face and the angry tapping of her foot.

"Is something wrong, my dear?"

"SOMETHING WRONG?" Raquella shouted. "What were you doing up there? You nearly killed me!"

The magician looked baffled by her outburst. "You were never in any danger. It's an automatic mechanism. As soon as the spikes come down, the straps are released and the table flips over, sending the volunteer down the chute. It's simple engineering."

"Couldn't you have told me that beforehand? And what was all that nonsense about 'no one comes late to my show'?"

"I'm sorry if I frightened you," Mountebank replied calmly. "The trick always works much better if the volunteer looks genuinely scared. It's all part of the spectacle."

"You'll have to forgive me if I am less than impressed." She gave Carnegie an accusatory stare. "Though it seems you have at least one new fan."

"It was a good show," the wereman agreed, oblivious to the edge in her voice. "I'm surprised you didn't have a bigger audience."

With a melodramatic sigh, Mountebank slumped down in front of the mirror and took off his gloves.

"Believe it or not, that was a good crowd. Darkside's the wrong place to be a magician. If it's not two animals ripping each other to shreds in front of their eyes, people aren't interested. They crave the bloody horror of reality. They don't care about illusions. They have no sense of . . . *wonder*."

He took off his jacket, draping it forlornly but carefully

over the back of his chair, and began to remove his stage make-up. "I don't know how much longer I can keep doing this. Eli Kinski is not renowned for his patience. If I can't get bigger audiences, I'll be off the bill."

"You could always introduce a bit more gore into your act," Carnegie suggested helpfully. "A few buckets of blood will bring the crowds in."

"Or," Raquella cut in, "you could listen to what we have to say. We have an idea that may interest you. A scheme that demands a man of your undoubted talents."

Mountebank leant back in his chair. "I'm listening."

Raquella took a deep breath. "We have to carry out a robbery, but we need help to pull it off. Specifically, the Troupe's help."

The magician laughed harshly. "I fear you are somewhat behind the times. The Troupe is no more – Ripper be praised."

"We've spoken to Correlli," Carnegie interjected. "He's agreed to help us. He and a friend of ours have gone over to Lightside to get the rest of the team."

"Correlli's agreed to reform the Troupe?" Mountebank said with surprise. "With me as well?"

The wereman nodded.

"Then he must have fallen on hard times. There is bad blood between Antonio Correlli and myself that will never be washed away." The magician shook his head. "I'm afraid to say I cannot help you. I have my act to think about. I can't just walk away at the drop of a hat to plan a robbery."

"But we need your help! We're trying to steal an item of great value. . ."

Mountebank held up his hand imperiously. "That is my final answer. I will hear no more about it."

Raquella glanced at Carnegie, who shrugged. The maidservant adopted an innocent expression.

"Well, if that is your final answer, I suppose we should leave you to get on. Good luck with your show – I have no doubt that better times are round the corner. Do we turn right or left by the toilet door?"

For a brief second the cruel fire she had witnessed on stage rekindled in Mountebank's eyes. Then he lowered his head.

"Even a magician should not try to deceive himself. You say that you are hoping to steal an item of great value?"

"Greatest value," the wereman replied solemnly.

Mountebank gathered up his jacket.

"Then let us go and see whether the fire-eater has cooled down."

15

The Troupe were reunited on a blustery afternoon down on the South Bank, under the revolving blades of the London Eye. Jonathan was sitting on a wall watching Fray and Nettle amuse themselves by performing gymnastic routines for a crowd of onlookers when he caught sight of Carnegie elbowing his way through the throng. Raquella and a striking albino man in a white suit followed closely behind him. Jonathan saw Correlli stiffen at the approach of the stranger, and a murderous look come into his eyes.

It was a muted reunion. Only one of the twins came forward to hug Mountebank, while the other sidled closer to Correlli. Verv was too distracted by a plane zooming overhead to speak to anyone. Carnegie looked on with unfeigned contempt.

"'The best thieves in Darkside', she said," he muttered. "I'll believe it when I see it."

"Did you have any trouble persuading Mountebank to come with you?" asked Jonathan.

The wereman shook his head. "He's a thief. He's greedy. It wasn't too difficult. It's going to be harder to stop the fire-eater from killing him, though."

At the mere presence of the magician, Correlli's face was darkening by the second. Hastily, Jonathan stepped in and invited all of them to stay at his house.

In hindsight, it was a big mistake.

On screeching up the driveway to the Starling house, Verv had shouted with delight and immediately annexed the garage as his own. Unwilling to sit through any planning meetings, he preferred to spend time tinkering with his beloved cab. The floor was soon slick with grease and oil, and the air thick with the poisonously sweet smell of petrol. Every now and again, the garage doors reverberated to the sound of hammering, a revving engine, or manic laughter. Verv slept in his cab, only leaving the garage to quickly stuff food in his mouth.

Fray and Nettle had scampered up the stairs to claim the attic room, bickering and pushing one another all the way. Jonathan was amazed by the length and sheer vitriol of their arguments – the only time they stopped insulting one other was when they weren't on speaking terms. And yet, in the early morning, they forgot their differences and made their way up on to the roof, where they cartwheeled and tumbled across the slate tiles, lithe shadows against a brightening sky.

With Raquella occupying the one guest bedroom,

Correlli made a bed for himself on the sofa in the lounge. He was a caged animal, visibly fighting the urge to lunge at Mountebank. The fire-eater threw himself into organizing the robbery, turning the lounge into a temporary war room, lining the wall with secret photographs of the mansion and detailed maps of Kensington marked with potential getaway routes. At night, as a release, Correlli slipped out alone into the back garden to practise his fire-eating, punctuating the night sky with the crackling whoosh of flames.

Perhaps mindful of the danger to his person, or – as Correlli maintained – to avoid the threat of doing any heavy lifting, Mountebank fled to the safety of the study, where he joined Alain in the hunt for information on Cornelius Xavier. The two of them made for a strangely compatible pairing: Mountebank airily reading aloud, his feet propped up on a stack of books, while Alain earnestly pored over half-opened books like an archaeologist on a dig.

"Your father has acquired a really rather excellent library," Mountebank mused to Jonathan. "How did he manage to obtain so many books with references to Darkside?"

"It took him a long time," Jonathan said finally.

He didn't know quite what to make of the magician. Given Correlli's reaction, he was initially wary of the albino, but – aside from the occasional grand magical boast or rambling theatrical anecdote – Mountebank proved thoughtful, considerate company. He sat quietly in meetings, rolling a coin effortlessly back and forth across his knuckles. From time to time he would amuse himself by producing various objects seemingly from thin air.

"How do you do that?" Jonathan asked, as a tortoiseshell cat appeared from nowhere and settled into his lap.

Mountebank smiled and stroked the cat's back. "I couldn't possibly reveal how a trick works, young man. Suffice to say, all the greatest magic tricks rely on the same thing – the subtle art of misdirection."

Given the barely suppressed tensions and threats of violence amongst the Troupe, it was a surprise that Jonathan's biggest problems were caused by the people he knew best. Carnegie was in particularly ill humour, seemingly unhappy with Correlli's attempts to take charge, and took great pleasure in arguing with the "blasted candle-kisser". Having been persuaded to sleep on Jonathan's floor, the wereman spent the first night growling and muttering in his sleep, keeping his roommate awake until the early hours. Rising reluctantly the next morning, with dark circles hanging beneath bleary eyes, Jonathan saw that Carnegie had dribbled a small pond of drool on to his bedroom carpet.

Raquella was in an equally awkward mood. She had stormed out of the first planning meeting after Correlli had abruptly ruled out her having any involvement in the robbery, and since that moment had pointedly refused to do anything other than menial jobs. She carried around trays of food and drinks and ferried messages between Troupe members, glowering and perpetually biting back a sharp response.

Having spent so many years in a slumbering silence, the house struggled to contain this explosion of activity: the stairs creaked and groaned under the weight of people running and pushing past each other; the kitchen floor was splattered with sugar, congealed egg mess and chunks of raw meat; and out in the garden, the shed bulged with an ever-increasing stockpile of weaponry and burglarious gizmos. One afternoon the neighbours came round to complain about the noise, only to find Carnegie answering the door. They did not complain again.

It was Tuesday afternoon. They had been in the house for forty-eight hours, and there were only two days until Vendetta's deadline expired. Jonathan went into the lounge to find Correlli poring over a set of architectural drawings. Deep in thought, the fire-eater ran his fingers through his wiry hair and sighed.

"Problems?" asked Jonathan.

"You could say that."

Correlli pointed at the photographs of Xavier's mansion on the wall. "See those little boxes on the tops of the walls? They're motion sensors. Make a movement between them and you're going to have alarm bells ringing. Not only that, but the dratted security cameras cover every inch of the grounds, and the guards appear to be armed with a small arsenal. Really, I don't know how Lightside burglars make a living. All these newfangled security devices take all the fun out of stealing."

As the fire-eater shook his head at the unfairness of it all, Jonathan peered over his shoulder at the architectural plans.

"Is that Xavier's mansion?"

Correlli nodded. "I sent Verv down to the council office to get hold of them. I've yet to find a public official who won't become very helpful if you offer them large amounts of money. These are the photocopies."

"Well, they must be useful at least," Jonathan said brightly.

The fire-eater pointed at a small room lying underneath the house. "I'm guessing this is the vault. We'll have to work our way to the bottom of the building – without being seen, obviously – and then hang around while the magician gets to work on the lock. But the vault isn't the biggest problem, Jonathan. Nor are the motion sensors or the cameras or the guards."

"Then what is?"

Correlli counted off his fingers. "William Enigma; Lord Appleby; Heinrich and Hans Hands; Nancy Esposito."

"I don't get it," Jonathan confessed. "Who are they?"

"A roll-call of some of the greatest thieves in the history of Darkside. All of them tried to break into Xavier's house when he lived in Darkside, and none of them were ever seen again."

"Yeah, but you're the Troupe. You're meant to be the best thieves around."

"Don't you understand? These guys tried to rob Xavier while he was living in Darkside! He didn't have any of this technology back then. There had to be something else in his residence, something that protected his money, something that all these thieves couldn't get past."

"Something Darkside," Jonathan finished, the truth dawning on him.

Correlli nodded. "We can have all the plans and photographs we want, but we don't have any idea what's waiting for us inside this place. Chances are, by the time we find out, it'll be too late."

He was about to toss the plans glumly to one side when he stopped suddenly and cocked his head. Placing a finger over his lips, the fire-eater raised himself quietly out of his chair and crept across the lounge. He whipped the door open, revealing a flushed Raquella standing out in the hallway.

"You could have just come in," he said drily. "Or has all that time at Vendetta's made eavesdropping a habit?"

"Certainly not!" the maid replied indignantly. "I simply came down to tell Jonathan that his father wants to see him in the study. It is clear that you see me as nothing more than a maid – I wouldn't dare to presume a greater role."

She glared at Correlli, daring him to demur. Unwilling to get caught up in the stand-off, Jonathan fled from the lounge and went up to the study, where the stuffy atmosphere was edged with excitement. Alain and Mountebank were hunched over a book, talking in hushed tones.

"What's up, Dad?"

"Jonathan, come in!" Alain grinned. "I told you I'd heard the name Cornelius Xavier before. Well, with the help of Mr Mountebank here . . ." (the magician sketched out a theatrical bow) ". . . I've managed to track him down."

He handed Jonathan a battered book entitled *Tales from the Whitechapel Gazette*.

"It's a collection of articles from a local newspaper that ran at the end of the nineteenth century, around the time Darkside was founded. It's packed with crazy stuff about conspiracies and monsters – probably why most people don't take it seriously. Some of us, however, know better."

He winked. Jonathan pulled up a chair and began to read the article, which was dated 23rd February, 1895.

Today the Whitechapel Gazette is the bearer of grim tidings for this fair capital city. One of its intrepid reporters has uncovered a scandalous situation at the Spitalfields lodgings of the notorious silk merchant Cornelius Xavier that will revile all right-minded Londoners. Born on the 11th December, 1861, Xavier rose to prominence as the purveyor of the finest silks this side of the Orient, but the Whitechapel Gazette can reveal that his business is based on cruelty, inhumanity, and an utter lack of the notions of human spirit and common decency upon which the British Empire was founded.

Two days ago a reporter secretly gained entry to Mr Xavier's workplace, an unassuming building in the heart of Spitalfields. A hardened reporter who has witnessed many of London's less salubrious sights, even he was shocked by the scene before him. Inside the main hall of the building were rows and rows of grubby, undernourished children dressed – if that is indeed the correct term – in filthy rags. They were tending to the giant silk looms that clattered ceaselessly, their hands darting in and out of the weaving like wasps in a flowerbed.

At the centre of this cacophonous pandemonium was Xavier himself, who scuttled up and down the aisles in a frenzy, a thick cane in his hands, exhorting his workforce to work faster and beating those unfortunates who were unable to comply. Whilst endeavouring to keep out of sight of Xavier, the reporter tried to speak to several urchins. Most were too weak from hunger and privation to form anything bar the most pitiful of complaints, or to utter the plaintive cry of "Help". Some were dumb with shock. One child was lying unconscious in the aisle, an ugly bruise on his forehead; none of his friends could break from their work to come to his aid.

When pressed to comment upon this foul

spectacle of inhumanity, Mr Xavier refused to talk to our reporter. The Whitechapel Gazette *urges the police to act swiftly in saving these unfortunate children, and displaying to Mr Cornelius Xavier the uncompromising and unimpeachable principles of the British justice system.*

"It appears that our Mr Xavier was not a pleasant man," Alain said mildly. "Anyway, according to a later piece in the book, this article incensed the local population so much that they burned down Xavier's factory and drove him out of the area, but not before he had vowed to go to a place where his work would be appreciated."

"And I think we all know where that is," Mountebank added. "Darksiders tend to be a little less squeamish about working conditions."

Jonathan couldn't believe it. The Cornelius Xavier in this book certainly sounded like the vicious man he had seen through the gate of the Kensington mansion, but the article had been written over a hundred years ago!

"But this can't be the same guy as the one I saw," Jonathan protested. "He'd be ancient!"

Mountebank smiled faintly. "Well, as you should know by now, Jonathan, things work a little bit differently in Darkside. This is Xavier, all right."

"Well, OK," Jonathan continued, "it's good that you found something on him, but . . . it doesn't really help us, does it?"

Alain's face fell. "Well, this is just the start," he said, a little wounded. "From here I can cross-reference to other works – we're bound to turn up something you can use."

The three of them dove into the books with renewed enthusiasm, leafing through dried-out pages of old journals and diaries. But after two hours, all Jonathan seemed to have picked up was eyestrain. He rubbed his face wearily.

The door to the study flew open, and Correlli burst into the room, a grim look on his face. Mountebank took a hasty step back behind a table.

"We've got a problem," the fire-eater reported.

"What is it now?" Jonathan asked. "Are the twins fighting again?"

"It's worse than that. Raquella's gone. And I think I know where."

16

In the end, it had been surprisingly easy. Raquella had taken advantage of a particularly tumultuous argument between Fray and Nettle to slip out of the house and catch a bus down to Kensington. Though she may have been touchy about the subject around Jonathan, Raquella had spent more than enough time on Lightside to get around without any problems.

Within an hour she was walking briskly along Slavia Avenue, her footsteps echoing down the deserted road. Although the light was fading and she was alone, Raquella wasn't scared. She had walked the horrific rooms and hallways of Vendetta Heights. It would take more than a quiet street to unsettle her. Maybe she should have felt more nervous – after all, there were no guarantees that what she was planning to do would succeed. But Raquella was certain she was doing the right thing; she had heard what Corelli had said back at the house, that the Troupe desperately needed to know what lay within Xavier's mansion. And she knew that only one person stood a chance of getting in through the front door: her.

But, if she was being honest with herself, Raquella had to admit that there was more to it than that. She was still fuming that Correlli had refused to allow her to take part in the robbery, despite the fact that she had survived Slattern Gardens and the Sepia Rooms in the past five days alone. The fire-eater clearly thought that she couldn't take care of herself.

In the past, maybe this wouldn't have rankled, but things had changed. For years Raquella had worked under the cruel whim of Vendetta, constantly reminded of the fact that her life hung by a thread. Well, now he had tossed her to one side like a broken toy, and she would be damned if she was going to sit on the sidelines while Jonathan and the rest of the Troupe decided her future. This was her choice; now *she* was in control of events. At the very least, her reconnaissance would give the Troupe a better chance of completing their mission. And who knew – if the opportunity presented itself, maybe she could steal the Crimson Stone herself. Raquella allowed herself a little smile at that thought.

The Xavier mansion was eerily resplendent in darkness, shadows settling comfortably on every twisted surface. The wind rustled conspiratorially through the trees. Raquella marched up to the front gate and buzzed the intercom. There was a lengthy pause, and then a voice crackled out through the speakers.

"What?"

"Please, sir, I have brought a message for Mr Cornelius Xavier."

"Mr Xavier isn't interested. Go away."

"But, sir," Raquella protested. "This is a very important message. From my master, Vendetta."

She waited, holding her breath. Then there came another buzzing noise, and the gate clicked open. Raquella stepped carefully up the driveway and knocked on the front door, adopting the dutiful, eyes-down demeanour of a maidservant.

A tall man in a black suit opened the door.

"You from Vendetta?" he asked brusquely.

"Yes, sir. Is Mr Xavier at home?"

"Mr Xavier is always at home."

The butler pushed the door open wider and beckoned her to come inside. Keeping her head respectfully lowered, Raquella passed into the Xavier mansion. The butler led her through a darkened reception area and down a long corridor. She looked around in the hope of spotting any secret security devices, but heavy blinds were drawn across the window, and it took her eyes time to acclimatize to the darkness. At the end of the corridor, a crack of light peeked through a door standing ajar.

"Mr Xavier is in the drawing room," the man announced.

Raquella cautiously moved past him and into the drawing room. A single gas lamp illuminated the silk merchant, who was stretched out on a divan, his eyes closed. His skin was a leathery map of the depressions and canyons of extreme old age. His bulky, misshapen frame was covered by a luxurious purple dressing gown.

Raquella coughed politely.

"I wondered when Vendetta would try and wheedle the Stone from me," Xavier wheezed. "I have to say, I thought he would send bigger messengers. With guns."

The silk merchant still hadn't opened his eyes, and yet it seemed he knew exactly who he was dealing with. Raquella curtsied to disguise her confusion.

"My master bade me to pass on his congratulations on your recent purchase. As you know, it is an item that is very dear to him and he would dearly love to gain possession of it. . ."

"'Love'? Vendetta?" Xavier snorted. "I hardly think so. If you haven't come to attack me, then make your offer, girl. You are starting to bore me."

Raquella took a deep breath. "My master will pay double the price you paid at auction."

Xavier tapped his fingers together, and then rose awkwardly from the divan. Standing up, he was little taller than the maid. He shuffled closer towards her. Raquella stifled the urge not to take a step back.

"Double my price, you say? What a very generous offer. Sadly, I shall have to decline. The Stone has a certain . . . sentimental value for me."

Something about the way the man moved unnerved Raquella. He slowly looked her up and down, as a predator would size up its prey.

"Then there is nothing my master could offer to change your mind?" she tried, a little desperately.

Xavier didn't even bother to respond this time. He ran a furry white tongue over his cracked lips, still inspecting Raquella. The maid was seized by the urge to get out of the study, and fast.

"Well," she said hurriedly, "if your mind is set, sir, I shall have to convey that to my master."

Xavier tutted, and stroked her arm with a leathery hand.

"No, no, no," he wheezed. "You're going to stay here, where I can keep an eye on you."

Raquella tried to back out of the door, but Xavier's grip was tight on her arm. He smiled as she began to wrestle in his grasp. Then there was a loud clicking sound, and as Raquella looked up with horror at Xavier's face, she realized just what his special defence was, and how foolish she had been to come here, but by then it was far, far too late. . .

"I don't believe it!" Correlli raged. "Of all the stupid, hare-brained ideas! What the hell does she think she's going to achieve – aside from putting the entire job in jeopardy?"

It had been two hours since Raquella had disappeared, leaving behind only a pointed note explaining exactly where she had gone. Carnegie had wanted to go after her, but it was clear that the maid had enjoyed too great a head start to be caught. Feeling helpless, the Troupe had congregated around a garden table in the fading light outside the back of the Starling house. Even Verv had emerged from the garage, and was murmuring sadly to himself.

"That's my friend you're talking about," Jonathan said quietly. "She put herself in danger to try and help us. There are more important things than this 'job'."

Mountebank shook his head sadly. The magician was cutting and shuffling a pack of cards, his hands a dextrous blur. "Jonathan's right. She was only doing what she thought was right. Poor girl."

Correlli gave him a venomous look. "I'd stay quiet if I were you, conjuror. Maybe you made her disappear."

"Hey!" Nettle exclaimed. "That's not fair! Don't you dare try and blame him!"

Fray pushed her twin roughly in the side. "Stay out of it, Nettle."

As the atmosphere around the table took on a dangerous edge, Mountebank glanced up sharply at the fire-eater. "If there's something you'd like to get off your chest, maybe now's the time."

Correlli drew a dagger from his belt and moved menacingly towards the magician. Panicking, Jonathan leapt up and stepped in between the two men.

"Hey, hey, hey! Enough! We're meant to be on the same side! What *is* it with you two?"

There was a long pause as the two men stared at one another. Then Mountebank shrugged.

"He's one of us now. Do you want to tell him, or shall I?"

The fire-eater sheathed his knife and slumped back down into his chair. "When you asked me about the Troupe the other day, Jonathan, I didn't tell you the whole truth. There was another member of the team. Ariel. She was Mountebank's assistant back at Spinoza's Fairground, an extraordinary girl." Correlli smiled, shaking his head slightly. "What a thief! We could never have got the Baskerville Emerald without her. Only a contortionist could have squeezed through that tiny air vent and got into the strongroom. Only Ariel could have got out again.

"After the robbery, we went out to celebrate. I remember sitting in The Last Supper thinking that anything was possible, that we were more powerful than even the Ripper himself! I should have known it couldn't last.

"After dinner we returned to the safe house. I knew something was wrong as soon as I entered my room. I had locked the emerald in a safe in the wall, but someone had blown the door and the window was open. I raced up on to the rooftops to see Ariel struggling with a man over the emerald – the Troupe's very own safe-cracker. . ."

Correlli's voice was drenched with bitterness, and for the first time since he started speaking, he stared directly at Mountebank.

"I ran forward to help her, but it was too late. She screamed, and then she was gone. Good old Mountebank managed to keep hold of the emerald, though. I would have thrown it away in a heartbeat, if it meant keeping her alive. I would have thrown everything away."

The fire-eater looked down at the ground. Silence hung heavy in the air. When the magician replied, it was barely more than a whisper.

"Not a day has passed that I haven't thought back to that moment and wished that I had managed to pull her back from the edge. But, Antonio, I swore to you then and I swear to you today: I didn't blow the safe, and I didn't steal the emerald. You're right – Ariel was an incredible thief. So good she couldn't stop. That night I caught her climbing out of the window with the emerald in her hand. I was trying to stop her."

"You liar!" Correlli sprang to his feet, fists clenched. "Ariel would never have betrayed us! She would never have betrayed me!"

"I didn't want to believe it either," Mountebank replied calmly. "She was my assistant. We had worked together for years, before the Troupe even existed. But you saw her with the stone in her hands. Believe your eyes, if not me."

The fire-eater pressed his face close to the magician's. "I will never believe you. One last job, conjuror, and then you'd better hope you never see me again."

Correlli stalked back into the house, kicking his chair over as he went. Fray went after him, staring daggers at her twin. Mountebank dabbed at his face with his pink handkerchief, giving Jonathan a wry smile.

"As you can see, Antonio and I have singularly failed to resolve our old differences. He'll never believe me, no matter what I say. He loved that girl. And she betrayed him.

It's much easier to blame the albino." He puffed out his colourless cheeks and sat down.

"Great," Jonathan replied bitterly. "Raquella's gone and all you can do is fight amongst yourselves."

Carnegie cleared his throat. "Well, everyone's going to have to get along for the next few hours, because we've got a mansion to rob."

Mountebank sat up in his chair, startled. "Tonight? But we planned for tomorrow night . . . we're not ready!"

"Change of plan," the wereman growled. "The boy's right – Raquella's a friend. I don't know what trouble she's got herself into in that place, but I'm not going to leave her there a second longer than necessary. If you or Correlli or anyone wants to argue with me on that point, you're more than welcome. I've heard a lot about how good the Troupe is. It's time for you to show me. We go tonight."

17

8.15 p.m.

As the van slowly pulled up to the security booth at the end of Slavia Avenue, Jonathan could feel his insides churning. It wasn't the instinctive adrenalin surge that danger had thrust upon him in the past but the cold, sickening tug of his nerves. So much could go wrong that it seemed almost impossible they could pull the robbery off. At the forefront of his mind was Raquella. Though he could have screamed at her for being so impetuous, Jonathan couldn't bear the thought that she was in trouble, and that they might not be able to save her. He tried to ignore the thought that it might already be too late.

"Here – have one of these."

Jonathan looked up to see Correlli passing him a piece of chewing gum.

"Gives your body something else to think about. And don't forget to look hacked off, all right?"

With his flamboyant clothing hidden beneath work overalls and a bright orange vest, and a hard hat over his wiry hair, the fire-eater was almost unrecognizable. He had taken the news of the change of plan surprisingly calmly. His eyes were focused, and his demeanour alert – Correlli was at work now. He stopped the van by the booth, rolled down the window and hailed the guard inside.

"Evening, guv," he said, adopting a thick Cockney accent. "Got an emergency call-out on this road."

He lifted the identification card from the chain around his neck and showed it to the guard. Aware that the tag was a doctored version of one of his old library cards, Jonathan was relieved when the guard barely glanced at it. Instead the man checked a clipboard, eyeing the two of them suspiciously.

"I've got no record of anything here."

Correlli blew a great gust of air out of his cheeks. "Don't mess me around, mate. Number 146. Electricity's gone out. People round here don't like to be kept waiting. I had to come here ASA bloody P. Had to bring my lad with me, and this isn't his idea of a great Tuesday night either."

"Like I say, there's no record of it here," the guard replied dubiously. "I'm going to have to make a phone call. . ."

"Nah, I tell you what," Correlli said aggressively. "*I'll* make a phone call. To Number 146. To the Israeli Ambassador, who's got a video conference with the UN in an hour. I'll tell him, sorry mate, I can't get your power back on, cause some idiot at the gate won't let me up the bleeding street! You'll be out of a job by half-eight!"

The guard hurriedly waved his hands as Correlli picked up a mobile phone and pretended to dial. "No, wait . . . 146, did you say? I'm sure that's in order. Why don't you go on through?"

The fire-eater treated him to a beaming grin. "That wasn't so hard, was it? Thank you very much. We'll be in and out in a jiffy."

As Correlli pulled the van away, Jonathan realized he had been holding his breath. "That was a bit close, wasn't it?"

Correlli shrugged. "Either he let us through or I brained him. It's easier this way, though, I grant you."

He manoeuvred the van down the broad avenue, which was shrouded in the late-evening gloom, and parked two houses down from Xavier's mansion. Jonathan hurried out and began unloading cones and barriers from the back of the van. Within a couple of minutes, the two of them had cordoned off a small area of the pavement. After much deliberation, Correlli selected a hefty pick from their selection of tools and flexed his shoulder muscles. He was about to strike down on the pavement when Jonathan caught his arm.

"You are sure this is the right place to dig, right?"

The fire-eater considered the question. "Fairly sure. Now

stop mucking about and give me a hand – this hole won't dig itself."

And with that, Correlli smashed the pick down on to the pavement.

10.42 p.m.

Vegard Amundsen was in the middle of writing a speech about whaling when his secretary knocked respectfully at his study door. The Norwegian Ambassador put down his fountain pen and removed his glasses before answering.

"Yes?"

A broad-shouldered man in a suit entered the room, closing the door quietly behind him. "I'm sorry to disturb you, Ambassador, but there are two gentlemen from the police here. They need to speak to you. Apparently it's urgent."

"Well, you'd better send them in, Thomas."

The secretary nodded. Amundsen carefully replaced the cap on his pen, wondering what on earth the police could want to see him about. In four years in London, he had spent the majority of his time at official functions and parties, mingling with his fellow diplomats and giving the occasional talk. Hardly matters of national security. And he only had an hour before he was supposed to deliver this speech. Why did these things always have to happen at the most inconvenient times?

Thomas returned with a policeman in tow. The officer looked round the room, openly admiring the lavish décor and the oil paintings hanging on the walls. As the man respectfully removed his hat, Amundsen couldn't help noticing that he was an albino.

"Thank you for seeing me at such a late hour, Ambassador."

"That's fine – I was still working. Thomas, could you get us some tea, please?"

The albino smiled as the secretary withdrew. "Tea? I see you've gone native."

"When in Rome. . ." Amundsen replied, laughing. "Please, sit down. What can I do for you, officer?"

The albino took a seat, casually balancing his hat on his crossed legs. "I don't want to alarm you, sir, but we've just received intelligence that a gang of criminals are planning a robbery in the area. We're informing all the embassies in the vicinity, and checking that their security arrangements are in place . . . Ambassador?"

"Hmmm?"

Amundsen had been momentarily distracted by a faint thud from the other side of the building. Sternly, he told himself to concentrate. "To be quite frank, officer, I can't imagine we'll have any problems here. The Norwegian Embassy hasn't proved too tempting a target for criminals in the past."

"Even so, Ambassador, we're taking this intelligence very seriously. You have security cameras posted around the building?"

"Naturally – all linked to the control room on the second

floor. I also have a team of bodyguards patrolling the building."

The albino's pink eyes narrowed. "And how many are on duty tonight?"

"Just three tonight, and Thomas of course. I have a function to go to, I am giving a speech. . ." He gestured at the paper in front of him.

"I understand completely," the policeman said smoothly. "I won't detain you any longer than necessary."

A thought suddenly struck Amundsen. "Excuse me, but Thomas said there were two policemen here. Where is your colleague?"

"He's inspecting your peripheral security. No doubt he'll be along in a minute."

There was a loud crash from the other side of the door. Despite himself, Amundsen shook his head. Really, Thomas was clumsy beyond belief. That was probably the china tea set the Queen had given him now lying in pieces on the floor.

"In fact," the albino said, "that sounds like him now."

The door opened again, and another policeman walked through. This man was much taller and more unkempt. He was half-shaven, and tufts of hair poked out from underneath his hat. His shirt was hanging out from his trousers and there was a rip in his jacket. The albino smiled brightly at him.

"Three guards, and the secretary," he reported.

"All dealt with," the new man growled.

The albino turned back to the Ambassador and stared at him thoughtfully. The atmosphere in the study had assumed a menacing quality. Amundsen realized that something was terribly wrong. Never a man to be flustered, he drew himself stiffly up behind his desk.

"I demand that you tell me what's going on here," he said.

"I told you," the albino replied. "There's going to be a robbery in the area tonight. We should know – we're the ones who are going to do it."

"But . . . why?" Amundsen gasped. "What could you possibly want here?"

"Oh, we don't want anything *here*." He pointed over the ambassador's shoulder. "It's *there* we want to get into."

Trembling, the Norwegian ambassador turned and looked through the window at the brooding shape of Cornelius Xavier's mansion. The last thing he heard was the albino saying delicately, "Carnegie – would you mind. . .?" and then there was a footstep and something heavy landed on the back of Amundsen's skull, sending him spiralling away into the darkness.

10.47 p.m.

Correlli saw a light flick on and off inside the Norwegian Embassy and grunted with satisfaction.

"The building's secure."

Jonathan stopped digging for a second and looked up. "I knew Carnegie wouldn't let us down," he said proudly.

"It's not him I'm worried about," Correlli replied darkly. "How's that hole coming on?"

Jonathan inspected the small crater they had dug in the pavement. "Shouldn't be much deeper now. In fact. . ." He stabbed his spade down into the earth, and there was a dull ringing noise. "I think we're there."

The fire-eater inspected his watch. "Just in time. Verv's going to be here in a few minutes. Here, let me do this."

Correlli hauled Jonathan out of the hole and dropped down into it. He spat on his hands and lofted the pick into the air.

"Let's hope we're in the right spot. . ." he said, and brought the pick down with an almighty clang.

Immediately the surrounding streetlights blinked with surprise and then went out, bathing the road in darkness. In the faint glow of the lights on the traffic cones, Jonathan saw Correlli shrug.

"You were only meant to knock out Xavier's place!" Jonathan hissed.

"Better safe than sorry," said Correlli, scrambling out of the hole. "Time to get inside."

10.50 p.m.

One of the twins opened the door to the Norwegian Embassy – whether Fray or Nettle, Jonathan couldn't be sure. As she was dressed in a jet-black bodysuit, complete with balaclava, it was difficult to make her out at all in the darkness. On seeing the two arrivals, she curtsied gratefully.

"Welcome. We've been expecting you."

"Thank you, Nettle," Correlli said drily, pushing past her into the building and heading up the stairs. "Playtime's over, though. No more jokes."

Nettle made a rude gesture behind his back, and draped an arm over Jonathan's shoulder.

"I'd forgotten what a grump he can be. Takes all the fun out of thieving."

She was unusually friendly – giddy even. With a start Jonathan realized that she was nervous too. For some reason, it made him feel slightly better.

They hurried to the top floor of the embassy and through an access door that led out on to the roof. From this height, Jonathan had a panoramic view of the grand Kensington houses, all huddled together in the darkness. Mountebank, Fray and Carnegie had congregated in a small circle, dressed in identical black outfits – the wereman had even left his stovepipe hat behind. Carnegie glanced at Jonathan as he walked carefully across the rooftop towards them.

"I see you put the lights out."

"It worked, didn't it?" Jonathan replied defensively. "I don't think *any* security cameras in London are working right now, let alone Xavier's."

The wereman chuckled humourlessly and mimed a round of applause.

"Remember," announced Correlli, exchanging his overalls for black clothing, "after Verv's show, the police are going to be on the scene pretty quickly. Now, we know that Xavier's not going to let them in, but if they start poking around here, we're going to be in trouble. We've got twenty minutes maximum. We're coming out after that, whether we've got the Stone or not." He looked everyone in the eye in turn.

"Ripper be with you all," Correlli said finally, and went to stand by the edge of the roof.

10.59 p.m.

Xavier's mansion stood implacable in the darkness. In the grounds, torchlight beams swept back and forth as the guards patrolled the area.

Looking down from the rooftop, Jonathan felt sick with nerves. He swallowed and scraped his tongue across dry lips. Around him, the Troupe stood abreast, waiting. Jonathan was amazed to see Fray and Nettle silently hug one other.

"Do you think that Verv will be on time?" he whispered to Correlli, adjusting his balaclava. "It's just he seems a bit . . . you know . . . all over the place. He wouldn't get the time wrong, would he?"

Gazing hungrily at the building before them, the fire-eater said nothing.

11.00 p.m.

From the bottom of the road there came a squealing of tyres, and a dark blue car came flying up the street. Above the throaty roar of the engine, Jonathan was sure he heard a maniacal whoop of delight from the driver's seat.

"Here he comes. . ." breathed Correlli. "Ready?"

The car flew past the Norwegian Embassy, bumped up on to the pavement, and crashed head first into the main gate of the Xavier mansion.

18

The next few seconds seemed to happen in slow motion. There was a booming echo as the car ploughed into the gate, which buckled and wobbled but held firm. Cries of alarm floated up from the grounds of the mansion, and there was the crunching noise of footsteps racing across the gravel. Down on the street, the tiny, Mohicaned figure of Verv disentangled himself from the wreckage of the car. He tossed something in the back seat and scampered away, whooping as he went. Fray glanced at her sister.

"Light the touch paper . . ."

". . . and stand well back."

A huge explosion rocked Slavia Avenue, so bright that Jonathan was forced to shield his face with his hand. He looked back to see the car engulfed in a fountain of fire, and Xavier's guards taking cover near the front gate.

"Our turn," said Correlli. "We've got twenty minutes, remember? Don't waste a second."

Nettle dropped to one knee and hefted what appeared to be a small cannon on to her shoulder. Taking aim at Xavier's mansion, she pressed the trigger. With a whoosh of compressed air, a spike came firing out of the cannon, a length of steel cord trailing out behind it. With a satisfying thunk the spike bit into the wall of the building, just above a balcony on the second floor. Nettle tied the other end of the cable tightly around the chimney stack behind them, creating a slender, sharply inclining tightrope between the two buildings.

Fray tested the cord, checking it was taut.

"Not bad," she said, grudgingly. "I'll go first."

She attached a small device to the cable – a greased pulley that could slide along the cord – then slipped her hands through the leather loops that hung beneath it.

"See you down there," said Fray, and with that she launched herself off the building.

Even though the Troupe had told him all about the death slide, Jonathan couldn't help but be amazed by the sight of the acrobat swooping down along the cord and through the night, the graceful adjustments of her body belying the perilous nature of her descent. The slide took her over the perimeter wall and up towards the side of the Xavier mansion. At the last second, the brake mechanism on the cord kicked in, bringing her to a halt. Fray dropped down on to the balcony and gave them the thumbs up.

One by one the Troupe followed her down the death slide, until it was just Carnegie and Jonathan standing on the rooftop. Jonathan attached his own pulley to the cord, his hands trembling.

"You OK, boy?"

He nodded.

"Whatever you do, don't let go."

Jonathan laughed nervously. He put his hands through the leather loops and shuffled over to the edge of the building. It was a dizzying drop to the ground below. He thought of Mrs Elwood, of Raquella, of his mum. He looked at the Troupe waiting expectantly on the balcony. So many people were counting on him. This was no time to back out.

Jonathan took a deep breath and threw himself off the edge of the building.

Immediately his arm muscles locked as they took on the strain of his body weight. The pulley zipped effortlessly along the cord, sending him hurtling down towards Xavier's mansion. He wanted to yell but the air had been buffeted from his lungs. At this height the wind was a living, breathing entity roaring in his ears. As he flew over the perimeter wall, Jonathan tucked his legs up beneath him, fearful of the large spikes straining to catch him. The loops were cutting into his hands but he had to hang on.

Looking on to the street, he saw Xavier's guards swarming around the burning carcass of Verv's car. *The art of misdirection*, Mountebank had called it. If any of the guards had turned their heads and looked up into the night, maybe they might have picked out Jonathan's outline cutting through the sky. But none of them did.

Xavier's mansion was looming larger and larger, swallowing Jonathan up in its shadow. Now he could make out the ornate columns and windows, the elegantly carved balustrades, the gargoyles glaring at him from beneath the eaves. Onward he went, picking up speed all the while, until it seemed he was going to fly straight into the wall. Instinctively he closed his eyes.

There was a twanging sound as the pulley encountered the brake near the end of the cord, bringing Jonathan to a halt so sudden that it jarred his arms in their sockets. Stifling a cry of pain, he dropped down on the balcony, where several pairs of hands received him, silently patting him on the back and ruffling his hair. As Carnegie flew down after him, Jonathan inspected his red-raw palms. Mountebank had crouched down by his side and was working at the window lock. By the time the wereman had joined them on the balcony, he had clicked it open.

The magician carefully opened the window and the Troupe slipped inside. They found themselves in a spacious living room shrouded in gloom. It was just possible to discern a jumble of silhouettes in front of them, a heap of objects cluttering up the floor and the surfaces. Correlli pulled out a pencil torch and shone a narrow beam over the surroundings. Jonathan was surprised to see that the room was filled with all manner of antiques: brooding statues, china plates, silver cutlery, slender vases decorated with willow patterns. There was a stack of paintings by his feet. He picked one of them up: judging by the frame alone, it was old, and valuable.

Correlli's eyes widened beneath his balaclava. He let out a low whistle. "Look at all this stuff!"

Mountebank nodded. "Worth a small fortune," the magician whispered back. "Actually, worth a rather large fortune."

Carnegie ran a finger over a statue and held it up, showing a thick layer of dust on his black glove. "Doesn't look like anyone comes up here often, though."

Jonathan was confused. Why had Xavier bought all these items only to leave them out of sight? What was the point of buying something he didn't care about?

Fray made a small sound of displeasure. Something was tangled up in her feet. She held up a fine white strand of material.

"There's not just dust here," she said. "This stuff's everywhere – what is it?"

"Silk," Correlli replied softly. "It seems Xavier likes to remind his visitors how he made his fortune."

"Show-off," muttered Nettle.

They crept out through the door and down a deserted hallway. Antiques and statues were strewn about the corridor like litter, all garlanded with silk strands that glistened in the dark and ran off into the corners of the passageway. At any second, Jonathan expected an alarm to sound and the lights to flick on, but there was no sign of life anywhere. The only sounds he could hear were

Carnegie's ragged breaths, the tread of Correlli's shoes on the carpet, and his own thundering heart. Mountebank and the twins moved in complete silence.

Correlli led them on down the hallway, beyond the grand main staircase and towards a small door at the end of the corridor. He tried the handle and the door swung open, revealing the back staircase the fire-eater had singled out from the architectural plans. The Troupe descended down the wooden steps in single file, alert to the slightest squeak or footfall. The silence was so loud it hummed in Jonathan's ears.

By the time they had reached the ground floor, Jonathan's breaths were still coming in snatches, and his hands were still shaking, but he was feeling slightly calmer. He knew from the plans that the basement was just around the corner. They were close now.

There was a movement in the dark ahead of them.

"Guards – down!" bellowed Carnegie.

Immediately the twins backflipped into the doorway on their left, followed by a ducking and weaving wereman. Jonathan froze on the spot, but then Correlli – the professional burglar, his reflexes honed by years of experience – shoved him roughly in the back, and into a side room on the right. By the time the guards had levelled their weapons and begun firing, only one target was still exposed. Mountebank the Magnificent.

"No!" Jonathan screamed.

As the staccato report of gunfire filled the hall, Mountebank shuddered violently, small puffs of smoke rising from his body.

The magician clutched at his chest, a bewildered expression on his face. He took one step, then another, before his legs gave way and he collapsed to the floor. A pool of blood trickled out from underneath him, staining the floorboards red.

Jonathan raced blindly out into the corridor to Mountebank's body, senseless to the bullets whizzing over his head. He rolled the magician over, saw the pink eyes staring blankly up at him, before a pair of strong hands dragged him back into the safety of the side room.

"Are you crazy?" Correlli yelled above the gunfire. "You could have got us both killed!" And then, more softly: "He's gone, Jonathan."

"He's . . . dead?" the boy asked, disbelievingly.

The fire-eater nodded grimly.

"And we will be too, if we don't move. Come on – we can still get to the basement if we go through that door there."

He pointed at a door on the other side of the room. Jonathan knew that he was right, but the rest of the Troupe were pinned down in the doorway on the other side of the corridor, the walls either side of them studded with bullet holes. They may have only been a few paces away, but with the gunshots ricocheting down the passageway, they might as well have been on the other side of the world.

"What about everyone else? We can't leave them behind!"

"They'll find a way out. There's nothing we can do to help." Correlli grabbed Jonathan's shoulders and shook him. His eyes were fierce. "It's you and me now. We're the only ones who can get the Crimson Stone. Pull yourself together, or all of this has been a waste. Can you do that?"

It was all Jonathan could do to nod, relieved that his balaclava was hiding the tears running down his face. As the fire-eater hauled him off through the side room, he raised his hand in a farewell gesture to Carnegie. The wereman ripped his balaclava from his head, concern etched into his face. A mournful howl followed Jonathan as he stumbled through the door and into the hall beyond.

19

The main hall of Xavier's mansion was paved with black and white floor tiles, marking it out like a giant chessboard. It was a large, draughty space. There was no furniture, no decoration, save for more strands of silk coiled across the floor. The high arched windows lining the walls were imprisoned behind shutters, and the musty, murky atmosphere suggested that it had been many years since they had admitted light or fresh air.

Only animal instinct, a deep-rooted desire to survive, kept Jonathan going, made him place one foot in front of the other. He was still struggling to come to terms with the fact that a man had died in front of his eyes. Jonathan's brain kept replaying the moment Mountebank had been shot: the way his body had shuddered as he was sprayed with bullets; the vacant look in his eyes as he toppled to the ground; the irretrievable stillness of his corpse. He knew that these were images that would haunt him for what remained of his life.

Striding purposefully ahead of him, Correlli was a picture of merciless calm. He hadn't even flinched as Mountebank had been shot. Then again, he had hated the magician. For the first time in days, Jonathan was reminded what sort of man he was dealing with: a thief; a thug; a mercenary. How many men had Correlli seen die, he wondered, and how many at his own hand?

As they continued down the hall, the sound of gunfire died away, and all that could be heard was the echo of their own footsteps. Correlli wrenched off his balaclava and tossed it on to the floor.

"No point trying to hide now," he muttered, rubbing his sweaty face.

Jonathan followed suit, relishing the cool breath of air on his skin. "I can't believe it. . ." he said quietly. "They killed Mountebank. . ."

"It's worse than that," the fire-eater replied. "That blasted magician was our safe-cracker. I don't know how we're going to get the Stone now."

Jonathan stopped abruptly. "You don't care, do you?" he said bitterly. "He's dead, and you don't give a toss."

Correlli didn't break stride. "Only ten minutes left," he called out over his shoulder. "I'd concentrate on the job in hand if I were you."

Jonathan was tempted to leave the fire-eater there and then and run back to help Carnegie, but deep down he knew he had to carry on. There were too many lives at stake, and he couldn't bear the thought that Mountebank had died for nothing. Pulling himself together, Jonathan jogged across the hall and caught up with Correlli.

"This place gives me the creeps," he muttered sullenly.

"I know what you mean," Correlli said. "There's something not right here. I can almost taste it."

"Still no sign of Xavier. Do you reckon he might be asleep?"

"I doubt it," the fire-eater replied. "I'm not that lucky."

He came to a halt before a doorway, and tapped his feet thoughtfully. "According to the plans, we should be over the vault right now. So where on Darkside is it?"

Jonathan gazed around the empty hall. "Do you think there's some kind of secret door?"

"If there is, I don't know how we open it. Unless. . ."

The fire-eater went over to the left-hand wall and began examining the plasterwork for a concealed switch, gesturing for Jonathan to do the same on the other side of the hall. As Jonathan crossed the floor, a hinge creaked, and he had to leap out of the way as a white tile beneath his feet swung open, revealing a set of steps leading down into the darkness.

"Er . . . I think I found it," he called out.

Correlli came over to him and peered down the steps, frowning. "What did you do?"

"Nothing! Just stepped on it."

"Less of a vault door than a trapdoor," Correlli remarked. "I don't like this one bit." He tucked his flashlight back into his belt. "No lights from now on. If there's something down there, I don't want them knowing we're coming."

Jonathan nodded, and hesitantly followed the fire-eater down into the gloom. He slipped down the stairs as quietly as he could, treading carefully in order to avoid tripping over the strands of silk that trailed down the steps. The air was getting hotter and more humid, like a greenhouse.

The stairs came out into a pitch-black space. Jonathan strained his eyes but couldn't tell how big the room was or whether anything was in it. He could barely see Correlli, and the fire-eater was standing right beside him. As Jonathan stepped forward, he had to forestall a cry of alarm as a silken thread brushed his face. The feel of the material against his bare skin set his teeth on edge.

"This stuff's everywhere," he whispered.

Correlli stopped in his tracks and grabbed Jonathan's arm. "Oh Ripper, no."

"What is it?"

Correlli didn't reply. There was a look of bewilderment on his face.

"Of course, *silk*. . ." he murmured to himself. "How could I have been so stupid? He's known we were here all along. . ."

"Correlli, what is it?"

He pushed Jonathan back in the direction of the stairs. "You have to go. Now."

"What? But we're so close!"

"Go, damn you!"

"What, leave already?" a hoarse voice rasped. "I'm afraid I can't allow that. . ."

Jonathan whirled round. There was a flicker of light, and then suddenly a lantern sparked into life, revealing the hunched figure of Cornelius Xavier. Up close he looked even older than before, his skin as dry as parchment and etched with deep lines. A voluminous robe struggled to contain his bulbous body. With a shudder Jonathan noted that Xavier's eyes were black holes, utterly devoid of any emotion.

The old man shuffled towards them with an awkward, unnatural gait. "You look surprised to see me. Did you not think I was expecting you? Or did you think I would go outside to watch your pretty fireworks? Vendetta must be losing his edge."

"How do you know about Vendetta?" Correlli demanded. "Did he tell you? Is this a set-up?"

Xavier grinned, revealing a row of blackened stumps. "No, no, no. Vendetta's desire to get his hands on the Crimson Stone is genuine enough. I merely had a conversation with his maid. I . . . *persuaded* her to tell me. She is a feisty sort. It took quite some time."

"If you've hurt her, I'll kill you," Jonathan said fiercely.

"Bold words, child," Xavier rasped. "The maid is still alive. She was lucky that I had eaten recently. But soon enough I will be hungry again, and then. . ."

Jonathan gasped. "Then what? What sort of monster are you?"

The old man laughed, wheezing like an empty bellows. "Monster? Children can be so cruel. Look around you. What sort of monster do you think I am?"

He clapped his hands and the room was suddenly filled with bright light. Jonathan stared around him, numb with horror. He was standing in the middle of a vast chamber, where the floor and the walls were coated in reams of silk threads, criss-crossing through the air high above his head. Together they formed a giant spiralling structure, just like a web. A spider's web.

Xavier laughed again. "Now do you understand? You walked straight into my lair, you foolish child, and now you're caught . . . like a fly in a trap."

There was a loud tearing sound, and six spindly legs burst through the sides of Xavier's robes. They flexed their joints and writhed in the air, revelling in their escape from imprisonment. The tatters of the creature's robe were left to stretch forlornly around the rolls of his bulbous belly. Somehow, the sight was made worse by the fact that Xavier's arms and head were still human.

There was a horrible sound of clicking bone, and the bottom of his jaw dropped down, widening his mouth into a hellish chasm. Xavier dropped down on to his spider legs, and suddenly there was nothing ungainly about his movements. He scuttled towards Jonathan, his feet clicking across the floor, his maw gaping.

"Run!" shouted Correlli, shoving Jonathan to one side.

Jonathan staggered away, not knowing where he was going. Blindly stepping over and ducking under strands, he headed for the heart of the web. Here the threads were as thick as ropes. He caught his leg between two strands and fell to the floor, the clatter of Xavier's legs getting louder and louder. Jonathan wriggled free and began crawling across the floor, nearly crying with desperation.

There was a familiar whoosh, and Jonathan twisted his neck to see Correlli, his back arched, a flaming brand pressed close to his lips. With a flourish, the fire-eater sent forth a wave of fire that made the web around him crackle and disintegrate. The chamber was filled with acrid smell of burning silk. With an angry chitter, Xavier abandoned his pursuit of Jonathan and scurried back towards the fire-eater.

Having been bought some precious time, Jonathan scanned the room for a weapon, anything he could use. Then, high up in the rafters, where the cobweb was at its thickest, he caught sight of a small bundle wrapped up in strands of silk. A single strand of telltale red hair had escaped from the top of it. Raquella!

Jonathan fastened his hands on the nearest thread and began hauling himself up, hand over hand. The silk strands were treacherously slippery between his palms, and for every two feet he climbed, he slid back down a foot. His knuckles blanched with the effort of clinging on. As Jonathan continued his torturous ascent, down on the floor Correlli aimed another jet of flame at the spider, which veered out of the way with frightening ease. The fire-eater was on the defensive, dodging and weaving through the cobwebs, and his brand was burning dangerously low. He couldn't keep it up for much longer. Focusing his gaze on Raquella, Jonathan gritted his teeth and redoubled his efforts.

The higher he climbed, the more tangled the cobweb became, allowing him to use his feet, as if he were scrambling up a net on an assault course. Though the going was slightly easier, the threads still wobbled dangerously each time he put weight on them, and he knew that one slip would send him crashing to the unforgiving stone floor.

Nearing the ceiling, Jonathan grabbed a thread running above his head and began to traverse the web towards the mummified form of Raquella, rocking forward and backwards as he struggled to keep his balance.

"I'm coming, Raquella!" he called out. "Hold on!"

Reaching the cocoon, he held on to it to steady himself. Even this close, the only sign of Raquella beneath the silk strands was the single lock of red hair. Jonathan frantically clawed at the cocoon, tearing handfuls of threads away until he could see her face.

"Raquella!" Jonathan said urgently. "Are you OK?"

The maid said nothing. Her face was drained of colour, and her eyes were wide with shock.

Suddenly Jonathan felt the thread he was clinging to shake violently. He looked down with horror to see the spider-beast clambering up towards him, an army of legs propelling its obese body upwards. There was no sign of Correlli. Jonathan's first thought was to flee, but there was no way he could leave Raquella with this monstrosity. He attacked the cocoon feverishly, succeeding in freeing the top half of the maid's body. Even though they had been released, Raquella's arms hung lifelessly by her side. She looked like she had been hypnotized.

"Please, Raquella!" Jonathan cried. "You've got to move! It's coming!"

A soft moan escaped from the maid's lips, but she didn't move.

Xavier was only a few feet below him now. Jonathan could hear the creature making excited clicking noises to itself. Where had Correlli gone? Coming to rest at an intersection of webs, the spider suddenly spat a stream of thick green liquid from its maw. A globule landed on the strand beneath Jonathan's feet, making the silk fizz and bubble. Jonathan began shuffling towards another part of the web, but it was too late: the thread gave way, and he felt his legs kicking out into thin air. He instinctively reached out and managed to grab another strand above his head, but he was left dangling helplessly in mid-air. Twisting his face into a hungry leer, Xavier went in for the kill.

20

"**D**rop, boy!"

The chamber reverberated with the sound of Elias Carnegie's gruff bellow. The wereman had burst down the steps and was now racing headlong across the floor. His black clothes were torn, and his exposed face was bleeding. In his right hand, he was carrying an antique spear.

Jonathan couldn't see the floor through the tangled mass of strands beneath him, but he knew that he was high enough up to make it unlikely that he'd survive the fall. The spider lurched closer towards him, and sent another venomous globule whistling past his ear. One thing was clear – if he stayed up here, he was dead for sure. He had to trust Carnegie.

"I'll be back!" he shouted to Raquella, and let go of the web.

As Xavier chittered in fury, Jonathan fell through the air, his arms and legs flailing wildly. After what felt like an age, he landed smack in the middle of a pile of off-white objects, which cracked loudly beneath him. Jonathan lay still for a second, unable to move. The impact had punched the wind from his lungs, and his left leg was in agony, but he was alive. Looking around him, he saw that the off-white objects were a collection of giant shells. He picked one up. It was the shape of a long insect's leg. His stomach lurching, Jonathan realized that his life had been saved by a pile of the spider's discarded skins.

He rolled gingerly to one side, as quickly as his battered body would allow, and got to his feet. Carnegie had crossed the chamber and was now shaking the bottom of the web beneath Xavier, trying to draw the spider away from Raquella.

"Come here, you overgrown bug!" he snarled.

By way of response, the spider spat forth another stream of venomous liquid, splattering the flagstones near the wereman. Then, without warning, it sprung off the web and dropped down from the ceiling. Carnegie had to roll out of the way as Xavier landed on the ground with a mighty thud, his many legs absorbing the impact.

The wereman took a step back, his shoulders shaking uncontrollably, and he dropped to his knees as the beast within took control of his body. Immediately the spider was upon him, knocking the spear out of his grasp with one of its legs and sending it rolling away across the floor. Carnegie howled with rage and aimed a backhanded slice with his claws at the creature's eyes.

As the two beasts clashed, Jonathan limped across the chamber and retrieved the spear. It must have been another one of Xavier's antiques: a simple wooden stick, covered in tribal decorations, with a sharp iron point on the end. Jonathan just hoped it worked as a weapon.

Though Carnegie was fighting like a wounded animal, Xavier's sheer weight and number of legs were overwhelming. As Jonathan crept back towards them, the spider succeeding in pinning the wereman's arms to his sides, encircling his legs around him like a ribcage. Carnegie stopped howling and eyeballed Xavier, daring him to finish him off.

As Xavier threw his head back and prepared to douse Carnegie in venom, Jonathan thrust the spear upwards into the exposed belly of the spider. The creature reared up with pain, emitting a high-pitched scream that was neither human nor animal. Thick green pus oozed from its wound. Xavier thrashed and writhed, catching Jonathan on the chin with a flailing leg. The boy went stumbling back, landing in a dazed heap on the floor. He heard another terrible scream, and then there was silence. Jonathan slumped back on the flagstones, utterly drained.

He opened his eyes to see a tall, dishevelled figure towering over him.

"Seems I owe you one, boy. You all right?"

Jonathan nodded, catching his breath. He pointed up towards the ceiling. "Raquella ... we've got to get her down."

"Leave it to me."

Carnegie swung athletically to the top of the cobweb and ripped through the remains of the cocoon with his claws. He bundled Raquella over his shoulder and descended back to the ground. Usually, the maid would have been furious at such an undignified journey, but she didn't snap or shout. She didn't, Jonathan noticed, say anything at all. The wereman set her gently down on the ground and lifted her chin so he could look into her eyes, which were bulging with fright.

"Is she OK?" asked Jonathan, hovering nervously over Carnegie's shoulder.

"She's in shock," the wereman replied. "Hardly surprising. She'll be better when we get her out of here."

Jonathan nodded at the spear protruding from Xavier's side. "Good job you brought that along."

"I found it in the umbrella stand on the way here – was the only antique that looked like it might be useful in a fight."

There was a clatter from the other side of the chamber, and Correlli appeared from behind the recesses of the cobweb, a flaming torch in one hand and a thick metal pole in the other. Carnegie bared his teeth angrily.

"Just in time," he barked sarcastically. "Where on Darkside have you been?"

Correlli spread his hands. "When my fire-stick went out I had no more weapons, and I wasn't going to wrestle that thing with my bare hands. I went looking for something big to hit it with. Looks like I wasn't needed anyway." Correlli dropped the pole to the ground. "Where are Fray and Nettle?"

Carnegie smiled sourly. "They decided they'd lead the remaining guards on a goose chase around the mansion. I think they're actually having fun."

"Which is great for them, but we're running out of time," Jonathan pressed. "We've got to find the vault."

Correlli jerked a thumb in the direction he had come from. "It's over there. I—"

"Rat dung!"

The wereman grabbed a fistful of Correlli's shirt, and pulled him so close their noses were almost touching.

"You weren't looking for a weapon, you wretched thief," he said, through clenched teeth. "You thought Xavier might be too busy munching on the boy to notice you waltzing off with his jewels!"

In the past, Jonathan had seen some of Darkside's most hardened criminals stutter and wilt under Carnegie's interrogations. But Correlli simply looked the wereman calmly in the eye, and said levelly:

"I'm telling the truth. I was looking for a weapon. I stumbled across the vault by accident."

"I don't believe you," Carnegie snarled.

Jonathan barged his way in between the two men, forcing them apart. "We haven't got time for this! Sort it out later. Look, me and Correlli will go and try to get into the vault. Carnegie, you have to get Raquella out of here."

The wereman shook his head. "Not leaving you with him. He'll double-cross you."

Jonathan pointed at the maid, who was still sitting on the floor, hugging her knees and whispering to herself. "Look at her! She can't stay here!" He pulled Carnegie to one side, and said quietly in his ear: "It's my fault she got into this mess in the first place. You're the only person I can trust to get her to safety. Please, Carnegie."

A guttural note of displeasure emanated from the back of the wereman's throat. "I don't like this, boy."

"You don't have to. I'll be fine, I promise."

Carnegie strode over to Raquella and swept her up in his arms as if she weighed no more than a kitten. Before he headed for the stairs, he flashed a dark look at the fire-eater.

"This isn't over," he growled.

Correlli shrugged. "Is it ever?"

The wereman spat on the floor with disgust and walked out of the chamber, leaving only the echo of his footsteps on the staircase. The fire-eater turned to Jonathan.

"Looks like it's just you and me left."

Jonathan nodded pensively. Despite everything he had said to Carnegie, he wasn't sure he trusted Correlli either. Now, with just the two of them alone, the fire-eater cut a larger and more threatening figure than before.

"How much time have we got left before the police get here?"

The fire-eater snorted. "Who cares? After what we've been through, I'm not leaving without the Stone."

He strode off towards the vault, using the flaming torch to burn a corridor through the cobwebs. As they passed Xavier's bloated corpse, Jonathan tried not to look at the river of steaming green slime still oozing from it.

Compared to the fantastical horror of the rest of the chamber, the vault was a model of modern technology. Built into the wall, it comprised a stainless steel door and a small electronic keypad. Correlli ran his fingers over the vault door, his face grim.

"Can you break into it?" Jonathan asked anxiously.

Correlli scratched his forehead. "Without Mountebank's explosives or the combination code, I don't know how. It's too sturdy for me to force it open." Jonathan flinched as Correlli smashed his knuckles against the steel door in frustration. "Ripper be damned! We were so close!"

He slumped down with his back to the vault and put his head in his hands. Jonathan didn't know what to do. Mrs Elwood was still in mortal danger, Raquella had been frightened half to death, Mountebank *was* dead . . . and all for nothing. They had come through so much, only to hit a dead end. If only they knew the stupid numbers to the combination code!

Numbers. . .

"Hang on a second," Jonathan said slowly.

His mind retreated back to before the robbery, before they had got the Troupe back together, to a time when he had been sat in Alain's study, reading a book on Xavier. He

dimly remembered reading the silk merchant's birthday –
11th December, 1861. Could that possibly work?

Jonathan tapped six numbers into the keypad –
111261 – and pressed 'Enter'.

And waited.

After what felt like an eternity, the vault beeped, and the
door slid smoothly open. Correlli cried out in surprise,
nearly tumbling backwards into the vault. He scrambled to
his feet and hoisted Jonathan up into a joyous bear hug, a
look of astonishment on his face.

"You little genius!"

"It was nothing," Jonathan said, laughing. "You know,
right place and right time and all that. . ."

He glanced into the vault, and his voice trailed off.

"Correlli. . ."

The fire-eater looked round, his mouth open. The size
of a small room, Cornelius Xavier's vault was bursting at the
seams with precious stones and gems: glittering diamonds,
burnished rubies, glinting emeralds, piled up like pebbles
on the shore. The vault shone like a dying sun.

Jonathan stepped into the vault, and trailed a hand
through a tray of gold coins.

"How much is all this worth?"

"Millions," Correlli replied, a note of wonderment in his
voice. "Millions and millions. It must have taken Xavier
years to buy all of this." He held up a pearl the size of ping-
pong ball. "Nice, isn't it? I might use it as a doorstop."

They both laughed.

"But the big question is," the fire-eater continued, "which one is the Crimson Stone?"

Jonathan pointed at a metal box placed on a table towards the back of the vault. "That's the presentation case – it must be in there."

They marched past all the other jewels and stood over the unassuming box. Jonathan looked up at Correlli.

"Do you think, before we take it, we could have a look at it?"

The fire-eater grinned broadly. "I think that's the least we deserve. You can do the honours."

His hands shaking, Jonathan lifted the latch on the lid and prepared to feast his eyes on the most precious stone in Darkside. Then there was a sickening crunch on the back of his head, and he was unconscious before he had the chance to cry out.

21

"**A**nd when I woke up, I was lying in a hospital bed."

A hush settled like dew over Interview Room B as Jonathan came to the end of his story. He took a sip of water for the first time that afternoon, eyes blazing with defiance. From somewhere within the police station, there came the sound of a fist hammering against a cell door.

Across the table, Sergeant Charlie Wilson was speechless. He had listened to the boy's story with mounting incredulity. Ghosts and goblins, stones with magical powers, an evil grotto hidden away in London . . . he had heard some crazy excuses and stories in his time, but this one took the biscuit. It was bad enough having to sit in this boiling room, without having to listen to some lad concoct fairy tales. As Jonathan recounted his battle with the giant spider, Wilson sternly folded his arms, a dark look on his face. Now he sighed and shook his head.

"Told you you wouldn't believe me," the boy muttered.

Wilson laughed incredulously. "Believe you? Of course I believe you, Jonathan!" His voice dripped with sarcasm. "You broke into a mansion with a team of crack circus performers to steal a priceless stone because a vampire was holding your friend hostage. How could I possibly doubt you?"

"It's the truth," Jonathan said stubbornly.

"It's nonsense, and you're wasting our time. We've gone over Xavier's mansion with a fine-tooth comb, and we didn't find a single thing that backs up your story: no fire-eaters, no dead magicians, no giant webs and – most importantly – no overgrown spiders. You know what they did find? A young lad unconscious in a vault in the basement of a dusty, deserted mansion holding a sapphire worth millions!"

"I didn't touch any sapphires!" Jonathan protested. "Correlli must have planted it on me!"

Wilson leant across the table and said, more softly this time, "Look, I don't care who you're protecting. Maybe it's a close friend, a family member even. Maybe you think that you're doing the right thing by hiding them. But you've got to realize that the sooner you *stop* telling us cock-and-bull stories and *start* telling us what really happened, the sooner your life's going to improve."

The boy snorted dismissively and looked down at his feet.

Detective Carmichael stretched and yawned loudly, straining the buttons on his ill-fitting shirt. He had dozed through Jonathan's story, his eyes closed and his head nodding back slightly. Only when the boy had mentioned his encounter in the zoo had the detective's eyes flickered open and his head cocked to one side thoughtfully. If he had been surprised by the ridiculous fairy tale, he had hidden it well.

"So, Jonathan," he said affably, "what's the plan now, then?"

The boy eyed him warily. "Plan?"

"Well, today's Wednesday. You've got a day left until your deadline expires. How are you going to save your friend?"

There was a pause, and then:

"Get out of here. Find Correlli. Kill Correlli. Get the Stone off him and take it to Vendetta."

Wilson rolled his eyes. "I don't think you want to be talking about killing anyone, son. You're in more than enough trouble as it is."

"I don't care," Jonathan said flatly. "He betrayed us. After everything that had happened, after Mountebank had *died* . . . he knocked me out so he could get his hands on the Crimson Stone. He was lying to us all along. I'm going to kill him."

Carmichael's eyes narrowed. "And how exactly are you going to find Correlli? He could be anywhere."

Jonathan shrugged. "I'll think of something."

"Better think fast, Jonathan." Carmichael glanced meaningfully at his watch. "The clock's ticking."

Wilson had no idea why the detective was humouring the lad, but it wasn't helping. For all of his vaunted reputation, if this was Carmichael's usual m.o., it was amazing he had solved one case, let alone hundreds.

The young policeman shuffled his notes wearily. "Look, why don't we take a break for a few minutes? It'll give you some time to think things over and decide whether you want to give us a statement – preferably about something that happened on Planet Earth."

There was a rap on the door, and a blonde police-woman entered the interview room carrying a jug of fresh water. She flashed Wilson a dazzling smile.

"Thought you might need a top-up," she said.

Wilson could have kissed her, and not just for the water. "Thank you," he said, his cheeks reddening slightly.

"Very thoughtful of you," Detective Carmichael mused. "We didn't even have to ask."

As she placed the jug on the table, the policewoman smiled at Jonathan. "Hello. Sorry it took me so long."

Wilson was wondering why she was bothering to apologize to a suspect when he noticed that a smile of recognition had stolen across Jonathan's face. By then, though, the cold barrel of a gun was boring into his neck, and it was too late to do anything.

"Either of you bozos move," the policewoman said coldly, "and Chuckles here is going to regret it."

Jonathan's eyes brightened. "Hello, Fray."

Wilson's jaw dropped with astonishment. "Fray – you can't mean. . .?"

"Welcome to Planet Earth," Jonathan said acidly.

Fray beamed with delight. "You recognized me!"

The interview room door opened slightly, and an identical voice came hissing through the crack.

"This is a prison break, not a chat show. Get on with it!"

"Go boil your head, you fat pig!" Fray hissed back.

"Better a fat pig than a wrinkled old prune. It's no wonder you haven't had a boyfriend in years."

"YOU COW!" Fray screeched, digging the barrel of the gun deeper into Wilson's skin. The young policeman gave Carmichael a panicked glance out of the corner of his eye, but the detective ignored him. He was watching the exchange with undisguised amusement.

Jonathan rose from his chair and tapped Fray on the arm. "Er. . . Can we carry this on outside?"

"Right, yes," she replied hastily, and then announced to the room, "Jonathan and I are going for a walk. Unless you want to be filled full of holes, I wouldn't try to follow us."

With that, the pressure on Wilson's neck disappeared, and he looked round to see Jonathan slipping out of the room. Fray was backing away after him, her pistol still trained on the young policeman.

"Good luck," Carmichael called out, as the door closed behind them.

Wilson waited for a couple of seconds until he judged it was safe to move, then sprang to his feet and hit the alarm on the wall. A deafening siren began echoing round the police station. Carmichael was shouting something at him but Wilson couldn't make out what he was saying above the din. He raced to the door and peered around the corner to see Jonathan racing away down the corridor, flanked by two blonde policewomen. As a group of officers hurried towards him, Wilson pointed at them and hurriedly barked out:

"The lad's an escaping suspect. Watch out – the women are armed!"

The officers nodded and went charging off after the

fleeing suspects. Wilson was about to follow suit when he felt a restraining hand on his arm. Carmichael rubbed his temples and winced.

"I wish you hadn't set that alarm off," he shouted. "It gives me an awful headache!"

"Sir . . . they're escaping! We have to. . ."

Carmichael watched Jonathan disappear around the corner, and then turned on his heel and began walking briskly in the opposite direction.

"Walk with me, Charlie," he called out.

Despite all his better instincts, Wilson obeyed. They walked in silence through the station, past the other officers haring to join in on the pursuit of Jonathan. Seemingly unconcerned, Carmichael headed down a flight of steps, past the cells and to the lowest level of the building. This far down, the insistent blaring of the alarm faded into a background hum, to Carmichael's evident relief. Wilson looked around in bewilderment as the detective led him past a series of doors – he hadn't even known that there were rooms down here.

"I don't understand, sir!" he protested again. "They're going to get away!"

"I should bloody well hope so," Carmichael murmured. "I've done everything but roll out the red carpet for them."

"Sir?"

"I mean, do you have any idea how difficult it is to dispose of a giant spider corpse?"

Wilson gaped at the detective. "What . . . you can't mean . . . the boy was telling the *truth*?"

The detective came to a halt in front of a door with a large "D" daubed in black paint, and gave Wilson a prolonged appraising stare.

"How long have you been on the force, Charlie?"

"Just over a year."

"You know, that might just be an advantage. I have a small team that investigates crimes of an . . . unusual nature. Just like young Starling's here. We're an unorthodox squad, and we have to keep what we do pretty quiet, but there's nothing like it anywhere else on the force. How would you feel about working with us?"

Wilson's mind was whirring. So little that had happened today made sense: first the boy's crazy story, then his superior's suggestion of some kind of fantastical cover-up, and now this mysterious invitation. The young policeman had a nagging sensation that working under Carmichael would involve more days like this.

"To be honest, sir, I'm not sure if I'm suited for this sort of work."

Barely listening to the reply, the crumpled detective slipped a key into the lock of Room D and turned the creaking handle.

"Fair enough, son. Before you make up your mind, though, why don't you come inside? There's some people I'd like you to meet. . ."

22

Jonathan pelted along the corridor as quickly as he could, trying to ignore the twinges of pain shooting up his left leg, an unwanted remnant from his fall in the Xavier mansion. Fray and Nettle each grabbed one of his arms and urged him onward, glancing over their shoulders at the officers giving chase behind them. The alarm bell was ricocheting off the walls.

"They're gaining on us!" Nettle cried out.

"Not far now!" her twin chimed in. "Come on, Jonathan!"

They skidded round the corner and stumbled up a flight of stairs, the shouts of the chasing policemen echoing up the stairwell. This wasn't like in the past, when Jonathan had run rings around officers in shopping centres and city streets. He wasn't bored. He wasn't looking for a bit of fun. He was breaking out of a police station, and if they caught him, everything was over.

Reaching the top of the stairs, Jonathan crashed through a set of double doors and found himself standing in the main reception of the station. A pair of elderly pensioners waiting for attention gave him a curious look. Behind the desk, a policeman was shouting into his walkie-talkie. He stopped and looked up with surprise.

"What are you waiting for?" Fray screamed at Nettle. "Use the magic ball!"

Nettle gave her a frosty glare, and then hurled what looked like a small marble to the floor. Immediately the reception area was filled with thick purple smoke and people began coughing. There was a rumble of footsteps as the pursuing officers followed them through the double doors, but there was no way they could single them out in the fog. Jonathan felt one of the twins tug on his arm, and suddenly he was limping through the automatic doors of the police station and clattering down the steps outside. He turned to see tendrils of purple smoke drifting out through the entrance, beckoning him back inside.

Oblivious to the open-mouthed passers-by staring at the scene, Fray ran to the edge of the pavement and gave out a piercing whistle. Jonathan pointed back at the police station and looked at Nettle.

"What was that?" he panted.

"Gift from Mountebank," Nettle winked. "Knew it would come in handy one day. . . Oh, you have got to be kidding me!"

Her face soured as a police van came careering through the busy traffic towards them. It swerved through a minuscule gap between two cars and pulled up at the side of the road, to a chorus of angry beeping. The driver of the van rolled the window down and waved excitedly through the window.

"VERV!" the twins screamed, for once in unison. The driver jumped with fright.

"What? You tell me get fast vehicle, I get fast vehicle." He tapped his chest proudly. "I get fast vehicle with *lights*."

He flicked a switch on the dashboard, and the blue light on the roof of the van began to flash. Looking over his shoulder, Jonathan saw the first officers staggering out through the smoke in the station.

"Let's go!" he cried.

He hobbled round to the back of the van and manoeuvred himself inside, Fray and Nettle hot on his heels. They had barely closed the door when Verv stamped down on the accelerator, and the sudden forward momentum of the vehicle threw them all to the floor. Jonathan lay flat on his back, catching his breath.

"Do you think we'll make it?' he asked.

Tossing her hat to one side, Fray ran a hand through her blonde mop of hair.

"We should be OK. Verv's an idiot . . ."

". . . but he's a fast idiot," Nettle cut in. "He'll make sure there's no one on our tail, and then we'll ditch the van."

Jonathan nodded. "I don't know what to say," he said gravely. "Thank you – both of you."

Nettle grinned. "That's OK. The big bad wolfman made us promise we'd rescue you."

"He's very scary when he gets the teeth out." Fray bared her teeth and made a low growling sound, and the twins fell about laughing.

"Where is Carnegie?' Jonathan asked. "What happened to you guys at the mansion?"

The police van continued to muscle its way through the afternoon traffic, with every minute distancing itself further from the police station. Every now and again one side of the vehicle would lift up into the air as Verv hurled it round another sharp corner, before crashing back on to the ground. The driver whooped and banged the steering wheel as usual, supplying the wailing siren noise himself. In the back of the van, the twins breathlessly recited their tale, their sentences so entwined and overlapping that sometimes Jonathan couldn't be sure who was speaking.

"After you and Correlli ran off we gave the guards the run-around for a while . . ."

". . . led them on quite the merry dance . . ."

". . . and then got out of the mansion and back to the getaway car as planned. Verv was waiting for us, and Carnegie was there with the maid."

"She didn't look so good. Like she'd seen the Ripper himself."

"We waited for you as long as we could, but then the police showed up and we had to get out quick-sharpish."

"The wolfman wasn't happy about that – made an awful racket on the way back."

"It wasn't until we heard on the news that a boy had

been arrested in the mansion that we knew where to find you. After that it was just a case of . . ."

". . . playing dress-up."

"Wolfman went off to talk to one of his contacts. Knows we haven't got much time left to save your friend."

"When they mentioned you on the news, he got very angry . . ."

". . . *very* angry . . ."

". . . and started swearing about Correlli, blaming him for everything going wrong."

"Carnegie's right," Jonathan replied darkly. "Correlli double-crossed us – knocked me out and took the Stone."

"I *knew* it!" Nettle cackled triumphantly. "I knew he was a big phoney. Did you hear that, sister? Your beloved Correlli ran off with the Crimson Stone!"

Fray shoved her roughly in the arm. "Shut it! You don't know that yet!"

Before another fight could break out, the van came to a shuddering halt, sending the occupants of the back flying forward into the wire mesh separating the driver from his passengers. In the front seat, Verv methodically flicked off the flashing blue light and turned off the engine.

"We here – get out time."

"Yes, thank you, Verv," Nettle replied acidly, picking herself up off the floor.

Jonathan limped over to the van door and scrambled down. Shielding his eyes from the sun, he saw that Verv had come to a halt in the deserted parking lot of a large industrial estate, in the shadow of a series of giant warehouses. Parched weeds poked up through the pockmarked tarmac. There was no one in sight. Verv jumped out of the front seat, slipped on a pair of large sunglasses and stretched like a cat in the sunshine.

"Good day for a drive," he giggled.

When Fray and Nettle joined them, they had ditched their uniforms for their usual clothes. Fray glanced down at her watch.

"We've got to meet the wolfman outside Baker Street station in an hour."

"You go ahead," Jonathan replied. "I've got to go back home first."

The twins shook their heads. "*Not* a clever idea . . ."

". . . it's the first place the police will go looking for you."

"Yeah, well, I'm going to have to risk it. I want to let my dad know what's happening. And I want to see how Raquella's doing. It's not too far from Baker Street – I'll be OK."

"Sure you don't want us to come with you?"

Jonathan shook his head. "Thanks, but people don't tend to notice me when I'm on my own. If I start walking around with you guys, I think I'm going to attract a bit of attention." He grinned. "I'll see you at Baker Street. Try not to fall out on the way."

By the time he had reached his old road, Jonathan was starting to question the wisdom of his decision. He was a nervous wreck. The buildings and gardens that had been such a reassuring presence throughout his childhood had now become havens for police ambushes. A wailing siren sent him scurrying behind a bush, until he realized it was several miles away.

Even the Starling house didn't look welcoming. Jonathan stared at the windows, wondering whether half of the Metropolitan police force was lying in wait for him inside. There was only one way to find out. He crept up the driveway and along the side of the house, holding his breath. The back garden was quiet – no one shouted through a loudhailer, no gunshots rang out. Jonathan slipped inside through the patio door, and found his dad waiting for him.

Alain was pacing up and down the kitchen, a television tuned in to a news channel. Although he broke into a smile when he saw Jonathan, the worry lines that had etched his face for so many years were prevalent again.

"I see you got out," he said.

"You should be proud, Dad. Your son's officially on the run."

Alain laughed abruptly, and then a sombre look crossed his face. "This won't be like last time, you know. They won't sweep this under the carpet. There'll be all sorts of questions. We're in a lot of trouble. I should never have let them talk me into this."

"But you did!" Jonathan replied. "And we both know why. We've only got hours to save Mrs Elwood. After that, I don't care what happens! I'll stay in Darkside for the rest of my life. I'll come back and go to prison. I'll even try and tell them the truth again – if anyone will believe me. But I can't spend the next few hours in a police station, not today, Dad. I *have* to go to Darkside."

Alain let out a lengthy sigh, and then nodded. "Yes – I know you do. I really shouldn't let you, but I happen to think you're right. We'll have to straighten everything out when you get back, though."

Jonathan grinned. "Scout's honour. How's Raquella?"

"Not bad," Alain replied, "considering the ordeal the poor girl's been through. She's in the spare room, if you want to see her."

Jonathan padded up the stairs and went into the spare room. The curtains were drawn, and the air was deathly still. Raquella was sitting upright in bed, her face bloodless and her hands trembling slightly. She opened her eyes as Jonathan came in, and gave him a wan smile.

"Hey," Jonathan said quietly, sitting down on the edge of the bed. "How are you doing?"

"I've been worse. What are you doing here?"

"I just wanted to check that you were OK."

"That's sweet," Raquella said. "But don't you worry about me. I'll be fine! You have to concentrate on getting that stone back – for both of us. I'm counting on you too, you know."

Jonathan squeezed her hands sympathetically and smiled. Raquella made a small noise of distaste. The maid inspected her palms, her nose wrinkled.

"Your hands are filthy! You've got muck all over me!"

"Oh yeah – sorry about that." He spread his hands out, revealing a coating of yellow grime on his palms. "I woke up like this, and I can't seem to get it off. Whatever it is, it's stubborn stuff."

Raquella smiled faintly. "Boys – you're all the same. Sam couldn't get it off either."

Jonathan stopped in the doorway, scratching his head. "Mountebank's assistant?" he asked, frowning.

Raquella nodded. "He was secretly trying out one of his tricks . . . The Exploding Death, I think he called it. His hands were covered in the stuff."

The cogs in Jonathan's brain began whirring furiously, and a series of images flashed in front of his mind: the magician's death, the tiny puffs of smoke erupting from his chest as Xavier's guards had sprayed the hallway; the way Jonathan had reached out towards the magician's prone body, exposing his palms to Mountebank's battered chest. And over the top of the images, the magician's voice, repeating the same four words over and over again: *The art of misdirection*. . .

Jonathan gasped and sat down. "He couldn't have!"

"What is it?"

Jonathan laughed with disbelief.

"It was all a trick," he breathed. "Don't you see, it was all a trick! He was never shot – he never died. It wasn't Correlli who knocked me out and took the Stone – it was Mountebank!"

202

23

Jonathan was saying goodbye to his dad when he looked out of his front room window and saw a small figure walking briskly down the driveway away from the house. He swore loudly and ran out through the front door, catching up with Raquella at the gate.

"Hey!" he called out. "Where are you going?"

The maid carried on walking. "I've spent enough time in bed," she replied, in clipped tones. "It's time to go home."

"But you're in shock! You need to rest!"

He caught her arm, and she whirled round angrily, her cheeks flushed with colour.

"Oh really! What about you, Jonathan? Wouldn't you like to rest? And how *is* your leg, by the way? I see you can barely put any weight on it. Shouldn't someone take a look at that?"

Jonathan said nothing. Though he had taken a couple of painkillers, his leg was still throbbing, and he felt like he had been running on the spot for a week. His body was working on autopilot, his brain trying to forget how desperately tired he was. As he stared down at the ground, Raquella rubbed his arm and said softly:

"I have to go back, Jonathan. Don't you see? If something goes wrong and you can't get the Crimson Stone, Vendetta will never give me my job back. My family depend upon me. Now, either I go back with you or I go back alone. It's up to you."

He would have loved to come up with a new argument or find a way to stop her, but Jonathan knew that it was wrong. It was the same with his dad – although Alain knew that Jonathan took risks, he trusted him to make the right decisions for the right reasons. It was part of the reason why he loved his dad so much.

"Come on, then," he said finally. "We haven't got time to be mucking around."

Raquella curtsied with a flourish. "As you wish. And fear not – if you get into any trouble, I'll rescue you."

And, despite everything, they both laughed.

Two hours later, and they were back on the hellish hubbub of the Grand, standing outside Kinski's Theatre of the Macabre. The stale and sullen daylight had stripped the theatre of any airs and graces it might have assumed at night, exposing the dirt-encrusted windows, the missing turret at the top of the building, the wind nagging at the fly-posters on the wall. It would be hours before the theatre opened and the first act crept on to the stage, and a heavy padlock and chain hung around the front doors. A puddle of yellow liquid dripped slowly down from the top step. Clouds were drawing in overhead, and Jonathan felt the first warm raindrop splatter on to the back of his neck. He turned and looked at Raquella.

"You sure you want to come in with me?"

Raquella nodded. "I've made it this far."

Given all that she had been through, Jonathan was amazed that she had made it at all. He had taken her to a crossing point Carnegie had shown him once before, a wild and windswept journey across Hampstead Heath. The maid tramped over brambles and through hedgerows in stoic silence, her face drawn and tight-lipped. Only at the moment of crossing, when the foul atmosphere of Darkside reclaimed her, did she allow a murmur of pain to escape her lips. By comparison, Jonathan had crossed so often in the past week that he had barely noticed the change in atmosphere. He was becoming ever more grateful for his mixed lineage, and the measure of Darkside blood that ran through his veins.

Though the crossing via the Heath was quick and close to his house, the presence of a gang of Darkside robbers on the wasteland on the other side had dissuaded Jonathan from using it more than once. This time he banked on the element of surprise, and offered up a silent thank you when he saw the gang congregating around a huge campfire, tormenting some other foolish travellers who had strayed into their territory. He and Raquella crept silently through the undergrowth past them, allowing the stench of booze and body odour and the raucous laughter to wash over them. Returning to the belligerent hustle and bustle of the Grand had been something of a relief.

Jonathan looked the theatre up and down. "Do you reckon he's in there, then?"

"Who, Mountebank?" Raquella frowned. "Maybe. I hope so. We're in trouble if he's not, aren't we? What about the rest of the Troupe – do you think they'll get here in time?"

It was Jonathan's turn to shrug. "Dunno. I told Dad to go down to Baker Street and tell them we were coming here. Depends how quickly they can cross, I guess. Until then, it's just us two."

There was a pause, and the two teenagers stood in silence as the passing crowds buffeted them. It seemed neither of them wanted to go inside. Jonathan secretly wished that Carnegie was standing alongside him. Or even Correlli, for that matter. Then he imagined the wereman giving him an exasperated glare and shoving him forward with a giant hairy hand. *We haven't got all day, boy. . .*

Jonathan took a deep breath. "Well, the front door may be locked, but this isn't exactly Xavier's mansion. I bet there's a way we can get in round the back. Let's go."

He led Raquella down the narrow alleyway that ran alongside the theatre, taking care to step over the piles of rubbish and rotting rodent corpses. He was mightily relieved when he caught sight of a smashed windowpane on the ground floor.

"Let me," said Raquella. "I've got smaller hands than you."

She rolled up her sleeve and slipped her hand through the jagged hole in the pane. Moving slowly and carefully, she reached down to the latch on the inside of the window and jiggled it free, before retrieving her hand. Then, with a smile, Raquella pushed the window open.

"I should stop spending so much time with thieves," she whispered. "I think it's starting to rub off on me."

She hauled herself through the gap and dropped lightly down on the other side. Jonathan followed her, wincing as he bent his leg, and found himself standing in one of Kinski's gloomy dressing rooms. Unlike Mountebank's cluttered quarters, this room was bare except for a dressing table and a stack of animal cages against the wall. As Raquella inspected the dressing table, Jonathan tapped on the side of one of the cages, only to jump away when a large rat went for his fingers.

"Ugh," he shuddered. "I don't want to see this guy's act. I hate rats."

"Er, Jonathan?" Raquella said, in an oddly strained voice.

"What is it?"

"I don't think the rats make it on to the stage."

He turned round to see a pale Raquella brandishing a poster that read *Susie Strange – Mistress of Serpents!* The girl in the picture was dressed in a sparkling pink leotard and had a broad smile across her face, despite the snakes coiled around her arms and legs.

There was a hissing sound in the darkness.

Jonathan stifled a yell and scanned the floor, his legs trembling. There was a movement underneath the window, a flash of scales, and he saw a long, thick shape slither slowly towards him. Raquella jumped up on to the dressing table and gestured frantically at him to join her, but it felt as if Jonathan's feet had been glued to the floor. He was mesmerized by the snake as it slid closer, its darting tongue and tiny, cruel eyes.

"The cages!" Raquella squeaked, her eyes wide. "Open the cages!"

Jonathan turned round and fiddled with the cage door with shaking fingers, aware of the smooth sound of the snake's underbelly brushing the floor. Just as he was opening the cage door, the rat rushed forward and tried to bite his fingers. In his haste to move away, Jonathan knocked the cage to the floor, and the rat went shooting out through the open door and huddled in the far corner of the room.

The snake paused delicately, weighing up this new option, before giving Jonathan a final malevolent glare and making off after the rat. They waited until the snake had cornered the rodent before racing out of the dressing room. Jonathan slammed the door behind them and leant against it.

"That . . . was . . . too . . . close."

They hurried away from the dressing room, determined to get as far away from the snake as possible. Before long the corridor broadened and sloped upwards, and they came out through a side entrance into the main auditorium. The hall was deserted, rows of empty seats watching the stage in silence. The clowns painted on to the ceiling wrestled and battled one another without an audience to spur them on. Jonathan was about to make his way through the auditorium and head backstage when he heard a loud scraping noise. Ducking down behind a chair, he saw in the glow of the footlights a young lad dragging a box across the stage.

With a sigh of relief, Raquella walked past Jonathan out into the aisle.

"Sam!" she called out happily.

The boy looked up, startled. He peered out into the audience, finally catching sight of the maid.

"Oh, hello, Miss Joubert," he faltered. "What are doing here? The theatre doesn't open for a couple of hours yet. I'm the only one here."

"Am I early? The back door was open," Raquella lied breezily. "It's just that I enjoyed Mountebank's show so much that I wanted to see it again. He is performing tonight, I take it?"

At the mention of the magician's name, Sam stiffened. "I'm afraid not, miss. Mr Mountebank's contract was cancelled a couple of days ago. I doubt he'll ever perform here again."

"Really? That's *such* a shame!" Raquella walked down the aisle and up the steps that led on to the stage. "Will he be performing elsewhere?"

"I, er, couldn't say, miss," Sam stuttered, taking a pace back towards the wings. "I think he may have retired from the business, at least for the time being. Says no one appreciates magicians any more."

"So why are you still here?" Raquella asked sweetly.

Sam gestured at the box in front of him. "He wanted me to put his props into storage. My master is very particular about his props."

"Could you tell me where Mr Mountebank is now, then?"

"I don't know. Really, you have to go. You shouldn't be in here."

"You're lying," Jonathan called out.

Sam jumped at the sound of the new voice. "Who's there?"

Jonathan strode up the steps and on to the stage. Frustration boiled in his veins, and at that moment he felt like shaking the truth from the other boy.

"Stay out of this, Jonathan," Raquella warned, as Sam shrank further into the shadowy wings.

"He's lying, Raquella, and we haven't got time for this. Either he tells us where the magician is now or I'll make him."

"No – please!" Sam cried, holding his hands up around his face.

The maid stepped in front of Jonathan. "Not another step!" she said firmly. "Threatening him isn't going to help."

Raquella took a step towards the magician's assistant, her arms outstretched.

"No one's going to hurt you, Sam, I promise. But you must understand, we have to find Mountebank. I know he's your master, but he's done some terrible things and we have to stop him before he does any more. You're a good person, I can see that. You must help us."

Jonathan was surprised to see the boy's shoulders shake as he started to cry.

"Please, Sam," Raquella said gently. "For me?"

The boy sniffed loudly, and stepped out into the footlights. Raquella's hand flew to her mouth in shock. Sam's face was covered in red, puffy bruises, and his right eye was swollen completely shut.

"I can't tell you anything!" he shouted, tears streaming down his face. "He'll kill me if I do! And you too! He'll kill us all!"

24

Sam slumped down on the box and put his head in his hands. Instinctively Raquella crossed the stage to comfort him, but he shied away as she tried to stroke his arm. The maid shot Jonathan a wide-eyed glance over Sam's shoulder. Jonathan didn't know what to say. Despite everything, even though Mountebank had deceived and double-crossed them, it was hard to believe that the softly-spoken magician could have been capable of delivering such a beating.

"Why?" he said eventually.

"He caught me practising one of his tricks," Sam sniffed, the words tumbling from his mouth. "He'd gone away and I didn't know if he was coming back and I thought it couldn't hurt if I tried The Exploding Death again but then he *did* come back and he saw me doing it and... He's warned me before about using his props – my master's very particular about them – but he's never been like this before. He's never..."

He trailed off.

"Oh, Sam," Raquella said gently.

Jonathan got down on his haunches and looked the boy in the eye.

"So where's Mountebank now?"

"He told me to gather up all of his props and take them to him."

"Where?"

"I can't tell you!" Sam said miserably. "If he finds out, my life won't be worth living. Mountebank will hurt you too, and I don't want that." He looked up at Raquella, his eyes burning fiercely through the tears.

"The boy doesn't need to tell you," a deep voice boomed from the back of the auditorium. "It's perfectly clear where the swine's gone."

Jonathan peered out through the footlights and made out a familiar burly figure striding towards them, his barrel chest adorned only by a red waistcoat.

"Correlli!" he called out.

The fire-eater nodded grimly at him as he climbed up on the stage. There was a nasty swelling on his forehead, and his jaw was set with murderous intent.

"You got here quickly."

"No thanks to you!" Jonathan replied indignantly. "Why did you run off like that? I thought it was you who'd knocked me out."

Correlli sighed. "You weren't the only one to get jumped. I got a glimpse of Mountebank before he hit me, and when I woke up the only thing I could think about was getting my hands on him. The police were already exploring the place upstairs, and I couldn't afford to get caught. Sorry I left you to it, Jonathan. To be honest, I wasn't thinking very straight." He turned and looked at Sam. "Mountebank's gone back to Spinoza's Fairground, hasn't he? Where we all used to perform?"

Sam nodded, wiping his eyes with the back of his hand. "He said something about selling a stone tonight, and that it was going to make him rich."

"OK," Correlli frowned, "so Mountebank's selling the Crimson Stone, but who to?"

A face came unbidden into Jonathan's mind. He shivered. "Vendetta. It must be. Correlli, we've got to stop him! If he gets the stone from Mountebank, we'll never get Mrs Elwood back!"

"Oh, we'll stop him all right," the fire-eater replied darkly. "One way or another, this ends tonight. I should have made that cheap conjuror pay a long time ago. He's not going to get away with it twice."

Jonathan fished a pocket watch from his trousers and consulted the dial. "It's half past seven now. How far's this fairground?"

"Far enough. If Mountebank's selling the Stone tonight, we need to move."

They glanced at one another, and then Raquella gave Sam's arm a squeeze.

"Are you going to be OK here?"

The boy struggled to his feet, hastily wiping his eyes.

"I'll come with you," he said. 'You'll need me – no one knows my master like I do."

"No," Correlli said, shaking his head. "There's enough youngsters going as it is. You look like you've been through enough today, son. Put some ice on that eye and leave us to take care of Mountebank."

Sam opened his mouth to argue, then appeared to think better of it.

"OK, but . . . Miss Joubert?" He drew himself up as the maid glanced back at him. "Take care of yourself."

Raquella nodded gravely, and then walked off the stage and away through the auditorium, leaving the young teenager alone in the gloom.

As the three of them made their way through the dingy foyer, there came the high-pitched squeal of a horse from outside the theatre, and then an almighty crash. Correlli smiled thinly.

"I was wondering when they'd get here," he said.

Jonathan didn't have chance to ask what he meant. The fire-eater swung a hefty boot and kicked the front doors of Kinski's open, before striding out into chaos.

Directly in front of the theatre, a large, horse-drawn vehicle had reared up on to the pavement, its front right wheel spinning crazily in the air. The main part of the vehicle was an elongated carriage, in which rows of seats could be seen through large glass windows. On the roof of the carriage was an exposed top deck filled with long benches. The impact of the crash had thrown many of the passengers from the vehicle, leaving one portly man hanging from the side, his feet scrabbling desperately for purchase. Two horses were prancing skittishly on the pavement, their reins tangled up around a lamp post. A crowd of Darksiders had formed around the scene. Next to Jonathan, two urchins were rifling through the pockets of an unconscious accident victim.

Jonathan glanced at Correlli. "What *is* that thing?"

"That, my friend, is a Darkside Omnibus. It's the safest public transport in the borough. Not as safe as walking or staying indoors, I'll grant you, but it'll take you where you want to go. And by the looks of the driver, as fast as you want to go to."

Jonathan saw a spike of pink hair jutting up from the driver's seat and a fist punching the air in celebration. He laughed.

There was a commotion from the downstairs compartment, and Fray and Nettle came tussling down on to the pavement.

"That was your fault! You had to tell him 'left', didn't you?"

"You lying snake! I told him 'right' – it was *you* who said left!"

Seeing Jonathan, they stopped pushing each other and raced over to envelop him in a large hug.

"You made it! After your dad told us what was going on . . ."

". . . we made it over here as fast as we could. Hijacked some wheels too."

Correlli loomed up on Jonathan's shoulder and greeted the twins. "Hello, ladies."

At the sight of the fire-eater, the twins recoiled.

"It's all right," Jonathan cut in hastily. "I was wrong – Correlli didn't double-cross us. It was Mountebank – he faked his death!"

"*What?*" Nettle screeched.

Fray cackled triumphantly. "Told you so."

"Am I forgiven?" Correlli asked, with a raised eyebrow.

Fray gave him a fierce hug, while Nettle sniffed a grudging welcome. Amid the hullabaloo, a grizzled head lifted itself slowly from behind the guardrail on the top deck of the omnibus.

"If you don't hurry up and get on this infernal contraption, boy," a low voice said ominously, "we're going to have a serious falling out."

"Carnegie!" Jonathan cried out.

As the rest of the Troupe and Raquella filed into the main part of the carriage, Jonathan scampered up the small flight of steps that curved round the back of the vehicle, and came out on to the top deck. Amazingly, a small congregation of hijacked passengers remained sitting on the right-hand bench: a huge man with a violent tic muttering to himself; a woman in a low-cut violet dress bearing a profoundly indignant look; and a gaunt old man with sallow eyes. On the other side of the deck, Carnegie was hunched down on the floor, gripping the rail behind his head and looking slightly green.

"Hello, boy," he said weakly.

"You don't look so great."

"Buses. Can't stand them. Now go and tell that harebrained driver if he takes any more corners like the last one I'm going to throw him off the roof and run him over."

Jonathan patted the wereman's arm sympathetically and clambered over to where Verv was perched at the front of the carriage. The getaway driver had changed back into a more sober, old-fashioned Darkside suit, which only served to throw his bright pink Mohican into sharper relief. He clapped his hands excitedly when he saw Jonathan.

"Back on the cobbles," he giggled, clattering his teeth together and bouncing round in his seat. "Just like old times! Where we going now?"

"The old fairground on the way to Bleakmoor. And Verv?"

The Mohican driver looked up expectantly.

"Quickety-quick, yeah?"

Verv snatched up the reins and geed the horses into life, his delighted war-cry louder than their startled whinnies. The omnibus crashed down from the pavement and on to the road, sending Jonathan flying backwards. Unable to control his feet, he was staggering towards the edge of the deck when a cold hand fastened on to him and pulled him back. Jonathan turned round to see the gaunt man staring at him oddly.

"Thanks, mister. I nearly went overboard there."

The man smiled, revealing a set of gums that were bleeding so badly they had stained his teeth a sickly red.

"We wouldn't want that, would we?" he breathed. "Lovely little morsel like you."

He lunged forward, fastening long fingers around Jonathan's neck. Jonathan tried to cry for help, but his windpipe was choked and it was impossible to make himself heard over the thunderous clattering of the carriage wheels on the cobblestones. Frantically, he waved his arms in an attempt to get Carnegie's attention, but the wereman's head was in his hands and he didn't look up.

Black spots were forming in front of Jonathan's eyes. He reached up and tried to prise the man's fingers from his throat, but his grip was astonishingly strong. The man smiled in hungry anticipation.

"Been waiting all day to eat," he breathed. "You'd better be worth it."

Jonathan's head lolled back as his oxygen supply grew weaker and weaker. His legs were feeling numb and he knew he had only seconds before he passed out. The wind howled and buffeted his ears, merciless to the last.

Suddenly the carriage tipped sharply to one side, as Verv swerved off the Grand at full speed. The gaunt man stumbled, sending the pair of them flying into the guardrail that ran round the circumference of the deck. Jonathan found himself looking down at the road, seeing the cobbles flying beneath him and the startled faces of pedestrians. With the fingers around his throat relaxing for a second, he summoned the energy to throw his shoulder into his assailant's bony ribcage, and was rewarded with an "oof" as the air flew out from his lungs. Jonathan kicked out, and felt his foot connect with a kneecap. The gaunt man screamed with pain, and slipped further over the edge of the rail. Still he refused to let go of Jonathan's throat. At this rate he would take them both crashing to the pavement.

From nowhere a large object came crashing down on the gaunt man's forehead, tipping his entire body over the side of the vehicle. As he fell, the man grabbed a desperate fistful of Jonathan's shirt; he had to clutch the rail to stop himself from following the man over the edge. For a second their eyes locked together, before the gaunt man's fingers finally gave way and he fell in a jarring heap on to the pavement.

Half on his knees, Jonathan turned round, expecting to see Carnegie standing over him. Instead the woman in the violet dress put down her umbrella, brushed down her skirts and sat imperiously back in her seat, but not before shooting Jonathan a warning glance.

"Any more mischief from you and you'll follow him over. Understand? I'm late enough as it is."

Too out of breath to reply, Jonathan nodded and slumped back down by Carnegie, rubbing his bruised neck. Spots were bursting in front of his eyes like fireworks. The wereman still refused to look up.

"Are we nearly there yet, boy?"

Jonathan rested his head back against the bench.

"I dunno," he panted. "I bloody hope so, though."

25

The omnibus continued on without a breath or a pause: a reckless, rattling juggernaut. As they raced from the crowded streets in the centre towards the outskirts of Darkside, the last light drained from the summer evening sky, and workmen began lighting the streetlamps. The houses cowered from the hidden dangers of the night. Despite the lateness of the hour, the air was still warm and cloying, and Jonathan was glad for the cooling breeze that whipped across the top deck.

On they went, until the streetlamps came to an end and the road broadened and began to incline into the darkness. Judging by the juddering of the carriage, the surface was even more potholed and uneven. Up ahead lay the winding descent to Bleakmoor, and as Jonathan looked to the skyline, he caught sight of a large animal padding amongst twisted trees. The creature threw its head back and unleashed a howling lament; Carnegie raised his head in answer, his eyes glinting.

"We here! We here!"

At the front of the carriage, Verv bounced up and down and pointed over to a large field, on which a makeshift village of tents and booths had been erected. Spinoza's Fairground was deserted and dark, save for the far end of the field, where a ring of burning braziers formed an honour guard around one of the large tents.

The bottom deck quickly disgorged the Troupe and a bewildered selection of passengers out on to the pavement. As Jonathan and Carnegie made their way gingerly down the steps, one with bruises on his neck, the other still nauseated, Correlli gave them a quizzical look.

"What happened to you two?"

"Don't ask," muttered Carnegie. The wereman pushed his hat up on to his forehead, and sized up the iron gates before him.

"So the magician's hiding in here, is he? This looks likes a suitably nasty little hideaway. Anything we should know about before we go in? I hate surprises."

Correlli shrugged. "The fair closed down years ago, and this place has been deserted ever since. I haven't been here since Ariel died. There are . . . too many memories. Mountebank knows it like the back of his hand, though, and there's no telling what he's been up to. In fact, I'd be very surprised if he wasn't watching us right now."

Jonathan felt the hairs on the back of his neck stand up.

He glanced around the fairground entrance, half-expecting to catch a glimpse of the treacherous albino.

"Very encouraging," Carnegie growled sarcastically. "I guess I'd better take the lead then."

He reached forward to push the gates open, but Correlli caught his hand. "Not this time," he said softly. "Not with this man. I will lead."

The fire-eater pulled a long, curved knife from his belt and prised the creaking gates open with his free hand. Then he led them inside the fairground.

Even in the half-light it was clear that it had been many years since anyone had entered the fair to ride one of the amusements or play a game. Overgrown grass and weeds grabbed imploringly at Jonathan's feet, while the wind sliced through gaping holes in the canvas tents. Peering at a passing row of stalls, he could make out faded signs caked with mud advertising games of Hoopla, Bullseye and Try Your Luck. The tattoo parlour was empty, the sketches of possible designs faded beyond recognition.

The Troupe trampled along the wide grassy walkways, eyes straining into the darkness as they sought out the magician. But Mountebank was nowhere to be seen. After ten minutes of fruitless searching, Correlli called them all together.

"At this rate it's going to take all night," he reported. "We're going to have to split up."

"Is that a good idea?" Jonathan asked anxiously.

"No – but we haven't got much choice. We're running out of time. Look, you and Raquella stay with Carnegie. The rest of us'll split up. If you see so much as a glimpse of Mountebank, shout out. We'll come running. And remember who we're dealing with here – keep your wits about you, and for Ripper's sake, don't get distracted."

The rest of the Troupe nodded, and went their separate ways.

Verv tiptoed past a row of booths, making engine noises under his breath. Away from the wheel, without a rein to tug or an accelerator to press, he felt bored. On foot, everything just moved so slowly. Secretly, Verv didn't really care whether they found the magician or not; he just wanted to get back to the omnibus and head out on the roads again.

"Psst! Verv!" a voice whispered. It sounded like Correlli.

The driver spun round, almost in a full circle. The voice had come from inside a small wooden hut with round eye-holes cut into the walls. A sign above the hut declared "Mistress Margherita's Menagerie of Freaks – Look Inside At Your Own Peril!" Verv ambled closer.

"Hey, bossman, what you doing in there?"

"I'm trapped!" the voice replied. "Look!"

Verv scratched his head. Correlli had warned them all to be careful, and now here he was trapped in a freakshow booth! It was a good job Verv was here to get him out of a jam. The driver pressed his eye up against the wall and looked through. There was no sign of the fire-eater, only a figure cloaked in darkness. Verv was about to ask who he was when the figure produced a watch from his pocket and swung it from side to side.

"It's a nice watch, isn't it, Verv?' the figure said softly. "Look at the way it shines. It's almost enough to make you forget about anything else, isn't it?"

Verv would have nodded in agreement, but he was too busy staring at the watch, marvelling at its gleaming silver surface and the lazy, easy swings it made through the air. Other thoughts – those of magicians and hostages, even those of speed – drifted from his head like summer clouds as Verv's world was swallowed up by a watch face.

Having fallen out over which direction to go in search of Mountebank, the twins went on in frosty silence, stepping lightly over tangled guy ropes. It was Fray who noticed the building near the fence with its open door banging in the breeze. She tapped her twin on the arm and pointed at it.

"I bet you he's hiding in there. Looks exactly like the sort of rat trap he'd feel safe in."

Nettle shrugged, which was the closest she came to agreeing. The discovery of Mountebank's treachery had put her in a fouler mood than usual, and Fray hated to think what would happen if her twin caught up with the magician.

"Listen," she whispered. "There's no telling what's in there. We need to come up with some sort of plan."

"Here's a plan – how about you stay out of my way?"

"Wait. . .!"

Nettle roughly shook off her sister's arm and bounded up to the building and through the door. Stunned, it took Fray a couple of seconds to run after her. She found herself in a darkened passageway with smooth walls. Stumbling onward, she found that the passage twisted and turned like a maze. Her twin was nowhere to be seen.

"Nettle?"

The lights clicked on. Fray gasped. A hundred Frays gasped back. Everywhere she looked there were Frays. She took a small step forward into what looked like the passageway, only to bump up against glass. Where she had come from and where she needed to go to was a mystery. She was utterly disoriented.

There was a movement in the mirror in front of her, and she saw Nettle staring back at her.

"It's a Hall of Mirrors!" Fray cried out.

Nettle clicked her tongue with disapproval. "I thought I told you to wait for me?" she said peevishly. "You have to follow me everywhere, don't you?"

Fray went pale.

"Oh, what is it now?" her twin snapped. "Do you want me to come and rescue you?"

From nowhere, Mountebank was leaning idly alongside Nettle. The magician grinned.

"Nettle!" Fray screamed. "He's behind you!"

Nettle turned, but it was too late: Mountebank roughly

clamped a rag over her face. As her twin began kicking and screaming furiously, Fray raced forward to help her, only to crash headlong into another mirror. Dazed, she wiped a hand across a forehead; it came away wet with blood.

Across the Hall of Mirrors, Nettle had slumped to the floor. The magician was standing over her body, openly laughing at Fray's desperate attempts to reach them. She would wipe the smile from his face when she got her hands on him. Fray crashed into another mirror, shattering it into a thousand pieces. She was bleeding heavily now, but she didn't care. She would break all the mirrors in the damn hall if necessary. Nettle was in touching distance now. With a high-pitched scream, Fray launched herself over her twin and towards Mountebank.

An arm stretched out from behind her and grabbed her by the hair, bringing her down to the ground with a savage thump. Immediately Mountebank's arm was fastened around her neck, choking her.

"First rule of magic, little bird," he hissed in her ear. "Nothing is what it seems. Now let's see if we can't clip your wings a little."

Fray felt a damp cloth pressed over her mouth and an acrid smell burning her nostrils, and with a sickening sensation she realized that Mountebank had got them both.

As he wandered through the dormant attractions, Antonio Correlli felt eerily calm, peaceful even. It felt as though a great weight had been lifted from his shoulders. He had spent so many years questioning what had happened between Ariel and Mountebank that fateful night. There had been times, bitter moments alone in bars, when he had almost believed the magician, that the woman he loved had double-crossed them. But now he knew the truth: Ariel had been murdered, and it was time to take his revenge.

It was primarily for this reason Correlli had split up the search party. He knew that Mountebank would come for him, and he didn't want anybody else interfering. So the fire-eater made no effort to creep about unseen – he strode down the middle of the walkways, a flaming brand held high above his head. Finally, as he was passing the tall, red-and-white-striped tower that housed the helter-skelter, he heard someone whistling high above his head. It was a familiar tune – the funeral march.

Correlli craned his neck and saw Mountebank leaning over the platform at the top of the tower, next to the opening of the slide, which was coiled around the tower like a snake. Having discarded his mask of civility, the albino's face was now twisted with hatred, and his red eyes burned with malice.

"How very typical," he called down. "Antonio Correlli, striding around like a baboon."

"Hello, Mountebank," Correlli nodded calmly. "Are you coming down or am I coming up?"

"I'd stay on the ground if I were you. It's awfully high up here, and I wouldn't want you to have an accident like your girlfriend."

The fire-eater grimaced. For that, he was going to make the magician suffer. Dark, violent thoughts racing through his mind, Correlli strode over to the ladder at the base of the tower and began hauling himself up towards the top. At the back of his mind he wondered whether any missiles would come raining down, but there were none. There was complete silence. Correlli emerged out on a rickety platform rocking in the wind, and was surprised to see that he was alone. The magician was gone. Looking out over the fair, he could see Carnegie, Jonathan and Raquella down by the big top, but there was no one else in sight.

The only way off the platform apart from the ladder was the helter-skelter itself. Correlli peered inside the black tube. Surely the magician hadn't gone down here?

A hand planted squarely in the small of his back sent him toppling forward into the slide. He landed heavily on his chest. The floor of the tube was coated with grease, and before he could stop himself Correlli was hurtling headfirst down the slide, every curve sending him barrelling into the walls. As he continued his descent, picking up speed all the while, the fire-eater dimly realized that the pipe had not stopped at the surface but burrowed deep down into the ground. Then he exploded out of the slide, and into an underground pit filled with dank water.

Spluttering wildly, Correlli battled to the surface. As he wiped slime from his face, he caught sight of Mountebank sneering through a small grille high above him.

"I'll be back for you when I've taken care of the others. Even you should have trouble starting a fire down there."

Then the magician was gone, and all Correlli could see through the grille was the night sky. He dashed his forearm against the surface of the water in frustration.

"Jonathan!" he roared. "He's coming for you!"

26

Carnegie's head snapped up as he heard the cry ring out over the fairground. Beside him, Jonathan and Raquella exchanged worried glances.

"That didn't sound good."

The wereman shook his head. "Knew we should have stayed together. Come on."

Carnegie began loping in the direction of the cry, the two teenagers hurrying to keep stride with him. The wereman's movements were becoming more feral, his eyes filming over, and Jonathan knew that Carnegie was teetering on the brink of another transformation. It was the last thing he wanted. There was no telling what Carnegie might do in his beast form, and right now Jonathan needed him thinking clearly. He looked around, hoping to catch sight of another member of the Troupe, but the only movement was a tatty flag blowing in the breeze.

They came out on a large expanse of grass by the entrance to the Big Top. To one side was a giant carousel consisting of a circular wooden platform with a cylindrical core of rusty cogs and gears rising out of its centre. Like other carousels, there were model animals hanging down from the ceiling on steel poles, but instead of brightly painted horses, the creatures were imps and goblins with bared teeth and drawn weapons.

"What's that?" asked Jonathan.

"The Melee-Go-Round," answered Carnegie. "It's a pretty vicious ride, even by Darkside standards. By the time it stops, only one of the mounts is safe. You'd have to have a screw loose to go on it."

As they drew nearer the carousel there was a hiss of steam and the lights flickered into life, casting a tawdry red hue over the ride, and a scratchy record of screams and shouts crackled out over the loudspeakers. There was a bang and a puff of smoke, and suddenly Mountebank was standing before them. At his feet was a large blue box with silver stars painted on it.

"Welcome to my fairground." He smiled thinly. "So glad you could make it."

"Pleasure's all ours," Carnegie growled.

Mountebank tapped the box with one of his feet. "You got here just in time to watch me hand a rather special object over to Vendetta. I took the liberty of taking the Stone out of its casket and putting it in something rather more suitable." His pink eyes filled with wonder. "It really is a most unusual item – not at all what I was expecting. I had half a mind not to sell it to Vendetta after all, but then he is making a most attractive offer. One that will allow me to live in the luxury I deserve."

"That's it?" Jonathan said bitterly. "All of this is just about money?"

Mountebank snorted. "This isn't about money, Jonathan. It's about *magic*. Don't you see? Don't you realize what you witnessed in Xavier's mansion? The most dangerous, most dazzling Exploding Death ever performed! Mountebank the Magnificent needs no stage to prove that he is the greatest magician in Darkside!"

As the albino's voice rose to a crescendo, Jonathan saw the only way he could get to Mountebank; the only hope he had of regaining the Stone. He laughed loudly.

"*You?*" he said mockingly. "The greatest magician in Darkside? That's a laugh. You should be a comedian instead."

Mountebank's eyes narrowed. "And what would you know about the mysteries and intricacies of the magical arts, young man?"

"Enough to know that Carnegie found you in a fleapit playing to three people. Not very magnificent, if you ask me. I bet I'm a better magician than you. And I bet I can prove it."

"You presumptuous imbecile," Mountebank said, through clenched teeth. "How dare you mock me?"

"Surely the greatest magician in Darkside would accept my challenge. Unless he was scared, of course."

With that, the magician snapped. "Mountebank the

Magnificent fears nothing!" he screamed. "I'll reduce you to a snivelling wreck, a messy pulp! What is your challenge?"

Jonathan flung his arms aloft in a flourishing theatrical gesture. "I challenge you to take part in my most death-defying magic trick: Jonathan Versus the Melee-Go-Round!"

Raquella gasped. The magician tried to laugh, but his eyes were suddenly uneasy.

"Forget it, boy," Carnegie rapped.

Jonathan ignored the wereman, and stepped forward to eyeball Mountebank. "Whoever wins gets to keep the Stone, and can truly call himself the greatest magician in Darkside. After all, that's what it's all about, remember?"

The magician pointed at Carnegie and Raquella.

"Those two have to wait in the Big Top. I don't want them trying to save you."

Carnegie growled ominously. "Why don't you take *me* on instead of the boy?"

"It's all right, Carnegie," Jonathan said. "It's up to me now."

The wereman grabbed him by the shoulders and shook him. "This is beyond foolish, boy. This will *kill* you."

"Don't worry," Jonathan replied. "I've got a trick up my sleeve too, you know."

"It's Jonathan's choice, Carnegie," Raquella spoke up. "He knows what he's doing. Come on."

She latched on to the wereman's arm and dragged him reluctantly over to the Big Top. Trying to look braver than he felt, Jonathan strode past the magician and up on to the wooden platform. Though he had tried to reassure Carnegie, the truth was he didn't have the faintest idea what to expect, or how he was going to survive. In the red glow of the lights, the mounts looked even more demonic. As he walked round trying to select one, Jonathan noted that not all of them were facing the same direction. Eventually he settled upon a glaring hellhound in the middle of a row of beasts, its neck twisting up and its jaws snapping at the sky. He pulled himself on to the back of the hound and wrapped his sweat-slippery palms around the metal pole.

In the meantime, Mountebank had placed the box containing the Stone on a ledge by the central cylinder. "Prepare to be dazzled!" he exclaimed, and pulled a lever jutting out of the engine parts.

There was a loud grinding sound, and the cogs began to turn. Jonathan felt his mount wobble and then shoot forward at surprising speed. As the ride started to revolve, he looked over his shoulder and saw Mountebank leap neatly on to a gnarled goblin travelling in the opposite direction.

Jonathan was just getting accustomed to the movement of the carousel when there was a rumbling noise beneath him. He looked down to see the wooden platform sliding back, revealing a pit of sharpened stakes. The pit was too wide for him to be able to jump off the ride and back on to the safety of solid ground. An icy feeling settled in Jonathan's stomach: he was trapped.

Mountebank was heading towards him, cackling with laughter.

"No getting off now!" he cackled as he swept past, and flung out his arms.

Suddenly a raven was flapping around Jonathan's head, pecking and clawing at his face. As the black wings beat about his head, Jonathan let go of the metal pole and held up his hands to protect himself. He felt a sharp talon slice his cheek, and a trickle of warm blood ran down his face. Crying out in pain, he flailed his arms about and managed to catch the bird a glancing blow, nearly overbalancing in the process. The raven cawed in protest and flew off into the night. Jonathan grabbed the pole in both hands again, breathing heavily.

"That was just for starters!" Mountebank called out, above the clatter of the machinery. "Now the fun really begins!"

There was a blast of steam and a loud whirring sound. Before Jonathan could react, a circular saw swung down from the ceiling, its serrated edges shining in the lights, and ploughed into the empty mount next to him. The saw bit into the wood with a high-pitched squeal, sending a spray of splinters over Jonathan. With a final triumphant scream, it sliced through the mount and swung back up to the ceiling. Jonathan went numb with terror. If he had been sitting there, he would have been sawn in half.

The ride continued its infernal progress, to a backing of clanking machinery and the never-ending record of shouts and screams. All around Jonathan mounts were falling by the wayside. In front of him the metal pole holding up a fat goblin simply detached itself from the ceiling, sending the mount crashing down into the pit. As he passed it Jonathan couldn't help but look down, and saw the goblin skewered on the razor-sharp spikes. He wasn't the only one having a close shave. A bright-red imp next to Mountebank suddenly exploded in a fireball, forcing the magician to duck out of the way.

There were only five or six mounts left now, including Jonathan's and Mountebank's. From deep within the carousel's mechanism, the gears ground again. The platform juddered and then suddenly began to revolve twice as fast as before. Jonathan clung on to his mount even more tightly as the fairground flashed past his eyes at dizzying speed.

"Not long now!" Mountebank screamed, with an insane cackle.

Jonathan felt a hot blast of steam upon his neck and heard a telltale whirring noise directly above his head. His time had come: the saw was coming for his mount now. Mountebank loomed into view, laughing manically, and Jonathan realized that the last thing he would see would be the magician's celebrations. He was almost within touching distance now. . .

As the saw swung down from the ceiling, Jonathan hurled himself from the hellhound on to Mountebank's mount, managing to grab hold of the pole and swing one leg over the goblin's head. The magician's expression turned from one of triumph to horror.

"Get off!" Mountebank yelled. "You're too heavy! You'll kill us both!"

As the goblin shuddered with the extra weight, the magician hurled a handful of powder in Jonathan's face. Jonathan's eyes began to burn as if they were on fire. Temporarily blinded, he swung an elbow and felt it connect with the magician's face. Mountebank screamed and clutched his nose.

The goblin listed violently beneath them, dropping closer to the pit of spikes. Tears streaming down his face, Jonathan looked around furiously for an escape. The only other remaining mount was swinging around towards them, behind Mountebank's back. He had only one shot of reaching it, and he had to ensure that the magician was occupied. Only one plan came to mind – the oldest trick in the book.

Jonathan looked over Mountebank's shoulder and shouted "Carnegie!" at the top of his voice, his eyes wide with relief.

The magician's head whirled instinctively round, only to see no sign of the wereman. Taking advantage of the Mountebank's distraction, Jonathan pushed himself off the goblin and leapfrogged on to the passing mount.

"Now *that's* misdirection!" he called out, as his mount flew away.

Mountebank moaned with horror as the goblin broke

off from its pole and fell down into the pit. The magician leapt upwards, his hands desperately reaching out for something to hang on to. He nearly made it. His hand brushed the ceiling but no more, and with a final, echoing wail, the albino tumbled down into the pit of spikes.

Jonathan slumped against his mount, fighting the urge to be sick. With only one rider left, the machinery clicked into a lower gear and the spinning motion began to slow down. The platform slid out and recovered the pit, sealing the mangled body of Mountebank the Magnificent in a spiky tomb. And with that, the Melee-Go-Round came to a stop.

Jonathan stepped down from his mount and walked over to the central core, his legs shaking like jelly. He picked the box up from the ledge and carried it off the ride. As he stepped off the carousel and on to safe ground his legs gave way, and he collapsed on to the grass. Out of the corner of his eye he saw a movement at the entrance to the Big Top, and then Carnegie striding across the ground between them. The wereman loomed over him, eyeing him warily.

"That was one of the craziest things I've ever seen. You are certifiable." He crouched down. "You all right, boy?"

Jonathan looked up. "I dunno. I'm alive, I guess."

"Mountebank?"

"He's dead."

"Are you sure?"

Jonathan nodded. The wereman patted him on the shoulder.

"Come on. Let's get this box inside the Big Top. Seeing as you've risked your life for the Stone, I don't want Vendetta getting any ideas about cheating us on the handover."

Carnegie scooped up the box in one hairy hand and hauled Jonathan up with the other. They only just managed to store the box in time. As Jonathan emerged from the Big Top, he saw, in the distance, two headlights cutting through the fairground, and the sound of a spluttering engine came into earshot. It belonged to the only car in Darkside. It belonged to Vendetta.

27

As the car drew nearer, Jonathan wearily gathered himself for one final effort. The ride on the Melee-Go-Round and the fight with Mountebank had taken almost everything out of him, but he knew that the danger was far from over.

As the car pulled up to the clearing in front of the Big Top, Jonathan saw Vendetta behind the wheel, clad in a long leather coat and driving goggles. Marianne was lounging in the seat next to him, shocking yellow hair flowing out behind her. At first glance they looked like a well-to-do Victorian couple out for a drive in the country, but when they drove into the torchlight Jonathan saw that Marianne was carrying a pistol in each hand, and there was a bloodstain smeared across Vendetta's cheek.

The back seat of the car was taken up by Marianne's bodyguards, the giant mute Humble and the bustling, hyperactive Skeet. On seeing Carnegie they reached down and pulled out long-barrelled rifles, training them on the wereman. The final occupant of the car, sandwiched in between Humble and Skeet, was Mrs Elwood. She looked haggard, and there were dark rings beneath her eyes, but she was alive.

Jonathan cried out with relief and ran towards her. "Mrs Elwood!" he called out. "Are you OK?"

She nodded quickly, her face drawn. Vendetta killed the engine and waved Jonathan back. "I wouldn't get too close if I were you, Starling," he warned, removing his goggles. "You wouldn't want one of us to get nervous and start firing, would you? Who knows who might get injured?"

Biting his lip, Jonathan took a pace back. The vampire stepped down from the car and headed round to the passenger side, where he proffered his hand to Marianne. The bounty hunter gracefully accepted, and stepped lightly down on to the grass. She was wearing an ankle-length gown that covered her arms and neck, and matched the colour of her hair. Catching sight of Jonathan, she favoured him with a beaming smile.

"I knew it!" she exclaimed. "Didn't I tell you, Vendetta? I don't care what that two-penny magician says, it'll be Jonathan who turns up in the end? Didn't I say that, boys?"

Humble and Skeet nodded solemnly from the back seat.

"It appears your faith in the boy is never-ending," Vendetta retorted sharply. "I can't express how happy I am you've been proven right." He glared at Jonathan. "I was informed that you'd be taken care of. That's another bet you've lost me, Starling. I trust that Mountebank is dead?"

"Put it this way," Carnegie growled, stepping forward. "He won't be doing any more card tricks."

Skeet jumped up in his seat and cocked his rifle.

"Muzzle your dog or I'll have him neutered," Marianne snapped, her playful air vanishing instantly.

"Wait! It's OK!" Jonathan leapt in, fearing Carnegie was about to lose his temper. He pushed the wereman back. "Look, we don't want any trouble. All we want is to get Mrs Elwood back, and that's it."

Vendetta raised an eyebrow. "Which brings us neatly on to the most important question of the evening. You may have killed the magician, but do you have the Crimson Stone?"

Jonathan jerked a thumb towards the Big Top. "It's in there."

Marianne glanced at Humble. "We're going inside. You two take care of the lady as arranged, yes?" She turned to Jonathan. "Any funny business in there and your friend dies, understand?"

Jonathan nodded and pushed his way through the entrance flap and into the Big Top. Huge rents in the canvas roof exposed the night. A moveable stage had been wheeled into the centre of the sawdust ring. Mountebank's blue, star-spangled box was resting on a plinth on the stage, surrounded by a ring of candles.

Raquella was sitting in the audience waiting for them. She nodded at Jonathan as he entered the tent, and then curtsied briskly as Vendetta strode in behind him. The vampire ignored her, his gaze transfixed on the box. He walked over to the stage and ran a hand over it, his eyes gleaming.

"Do you have any idea," he said softly, in a voice thick with desire, "how long I have waited to have this stone in my possession?"

"Then don't keep us waiting any longer," Marianne called out. "Open the box!"

The atmosphere in the Big Top crackled with tension as Vendetta unfastened the latches on the box. Even Carnegie leant forward. As the vampire snapped the lid open, the sides of the box toppled backwards like a house of cards, revealing no Crimson Stone, no priceless gem, no glittering treasure of any sort. In fact, the box was completely empty.

There was a pause as the onlookers struggled to digest this fact. Then Vendetta grabbed Jonathan's arm and shook him violently.

"Is . . . this . . . a *joke*?" The vampire was so angry that he struggled to get the words out.

"No!" Jonathan cried, completely bewildered. "I swear . . . Mountebank told us the Stone was in the box . . . He must have hidden it somewhere else."

Vendetta didn't release his grip. His eyes narrowed.

"Did you think we'd just walk away with the box without checking? Did you think you could free your friend *and* keep hold of the Crimson Stone? Tell me, Starling, did you get greedy?"

"No — I promise! I don't know where the Stone is! I thought it was here!"

"I'm not sure I believe you."

"Oh, put the boy down, Vendetta," Marianne drawled. "You're too busy rattling him to think. Look at him — he's gawping like a goldfish. He's just as surprised as you are. And Jonathan's hardly the type to gamble with a friend's life. He's only half-Darksider, remember."

Vendetta flashed her a dangerous look. Marianne sardonically batted her eyelashes back at him, utterly unfazed.

"It seems," the vampire said slowly, regaining his composure, "that this evening will not have a happy ending after all. Especially for your friend, Starling. You have failed to fulfil your side of our deal. I shall take particular pleasure draining the dwarf."

"You even go *near* her. . ." Jonathan warned fiercely, as Carnegie flexed his claws.

They were interrupted by a peal of laughter from Marianne.

"I do love it so when you boys play rough. However, it's not at all necessary. I told Humble to let the dwarf go when we came inside."

"You did what?" Vendetta's voice was as cold as a grave.

"I told him to let her go. I want the Stone, Vendetta, but I'm not about to butcher innocent women for it. There *are* limits, you know."

"We were supposed to be a team," the vampire said, through clenched teeth.

Marianne laughed incredulously. "You don't know the meaning of the word. All this talk of how much *you* wanted the Stone, how *you* failed to get it. Well, see how much luck *you* have finding it now."

"I see. This may be a moment you live to regret."

Vendetta stiffly adjusted his leather coat and strode out, flashing Raquella a challenging gaze. "I shall expect you in the car presently."

"As you wish, sir."

"Raquella, no!" Jonathan cried, aghast. "You can't go back to him. Not after all this!"

"I can, and I will," she replied firmly. "This is why I came with you in the first place. This is what I want."

"I don't understand."

Raquella gave him a sad smile. "No, I expect you don't. Maybe one day I'll get the chance to explain it to you."

With a final grateful nod at Carnegie – who grinned wolfishly in return – Raquella hurried out of the Big Top. There came the sound of an engine coughing into life, and then the car moved away.

Marianne sighed with satisfaction and turned back to Jonathan. "All's well that ends well, wouldn't you say?"

"I'm not going to thank you for saving Mrs Elwood," he replied defiantly. "This was all your fault in the first place."

"Perhaps. But what was I supposed to do? I wanted the Crimson Stone, but there was no way I could get it from Xavier." Marianne shuddered. "I *hate* spiders."

"You knew!" Jonathan gasped. "Why didn't you tell me?"

The bounty hunter airily waved a hand. "To be honest with you, it slipped my mind. I had complete faith in you, anyway."

Carnegie growled softly. "You push too far, Ripper. One of these days you may fall over."

"No doubt you'll be there to catch me," Marianne replied. "Until then. . ."

With a final twinkling smile, she was gone.

Outside, the heat was starting to evaporate in the night air. Jonathan raced over to Mrs Elwood and enveloped her in a fierce hug.

"I was so worried about you! I thought. . ."

"I know, Jonathan," she replied, in a small voice, her arms wrapped around him. "It's all right. Everything's going to be all right now."

"Come on," Carnegie said, not unkindly. "Let's get out of this place."

As they left, Jonathan took a final look at the Big Top and shook his head.

"What is it, boy?" the wereman asked.

"I still don't get it. We go through all that – fight Xavier and Mountebank, nearly get killed – and the Crimson Stone just disappears. I didn't even get to see it in the vault. I'm not sure if it was ever there at all. Maybe it is a myth."

Carnegie chewed on an elongated fingernail thoughtfully. "If anyone could make the Stone disappear, it was Mountebank. He was a magician, after all."

"I guess. Vendetta and Marianne aren't going to stop looking for it, are they?"

"Let's hope neither of them find it. If half of what they say about the Crimson Stone is true, it could make them even more dangerous than they are now. I think we can worry about that another time, though. What are you going to do now?"

Jonathan shrugged. "I guess first of all we try and find the rest of the Troupe and check that they're all right. Then I should take Mrs Elwood back to Dad's place."

The wereman gave him a pointed look. "Are you sure it's a good idea for you to go back to Lightside right now? Given what happened at the police station?"

"You know, I'd forgotten all about that."

"Oh, Jonathan," Mrs Elwood sighed. "What have you been up to now?"

"It's a long story," he replied. "It all started when I went back to see Dad. . ."

Epilogue

It was later, as the candles burned down to smouldering tips and the darkness reclaimed the Big Top, that there was a movement from beneath the stage and a figure emerged coughing and sneezing, a thick coating of dust in his hair.

Even now, Sam couldn't quite believe he had pulled it off. Following Raquella to the fairground had been easy, and Mountebank had been too preoccupied battling Jonathan to notice his apprentice watching from behind the counter of the coconut shy. Sam couldn't quite say why, following the magician's death, he had raced round the back of the Big Top and slipped underneath the canvas. He wanted to know that Raquella was all right, but at the same time there was another reason, one that was harder to define – a strange feeling that it was *his* turn to take centre stage.

When he saw the box resting on the plinth in the centre of the Big Top, everything fell into place for Sam. Having spent years coming to the fairground with Mountebank, he knew that there was a crawlspace in the Big Top that allowed a small person to slip underneath the stage, and that the plinth had a false bottom. Once in place, the hard part was carrying out the switch swiftly and in silence. When the vampire opened the box to reveal an empty space, Sam had to fight back the urge to punch the air and cheer. Mountebank had always said his apprentice could never make it in magic – but what could he say now?

However, as Sam hauled his prize out from underneath the stage, he felt his elation tempered by a much darker sense of foreboding. He had expected to see a delicate gem sparkling in the gloom; instead he found himself peering at a musty stone slab slightly larger than a brick. One of its corners was chipped and covered in a stain Sam could only assume was blood. This was the mighty artefact imbued with the power of Jack the Ripper, the priceless treasure his master had died trying to procure?

Sam picked up the squat weight and headed for the exit of the Big Top, his mind haunted by doubt. He had stolen the Crimson Stone – but what on Darkside was he going to do now?

Dare
to discover more?

For more information about Tom Becker,
future terrifying *Darkside* books and spooky
competitions and downloads just visit...

www.welcometodarkside.co.uk

We'll be expecting you...